The Mnemonist of Dutchess County

Josh Koenigsberg

A Samuel French Acting Edition

SAMUEL FRENCH

FOUNDED 1830

SAMUELFRENCH.COM
SAMUELFRENCH-LONDON.CO.UK

THE MNEMONIST OF DUTCHESS COUNTY was first produced by THE ATTIC (Laura Braza, Artistic Director; Ted Caine, Executive Director) at Theatre Row in New York City in February and March of 2013. It was directed by Laura Savia; the set design was by Julia Noulin-Merat; the costume design was by Travis Chinick; the lighting design was by Dave Upton; the sound design was by Stowe Nelson; and the production stage manager was Katie Kavett. The cast was as follows:

MILO MAZOWSKI	Henry Vick
G.H. HULIE	Brit Whittle
SAMANTHA RILEY	Jessica Varley
JOEY GIAMANI	Malcolm Madera
GINA GIAMANI	Ava Eisenson
TITO DAVIS	Aaron Costa Ganis

CHARACTERS

MILO MAZOWSKI – Recently fired Campus Security guard at Deans College. Has an unlimited memory. Literally. Also has a deep emotional well that he has no capacity to process without help. 30s, Male.

DR. G.H. HULIE – Head of the Psychology Department at Deans College. Easily excited by intellectual ideas. Extremely articulate. Tries his best not to be pretentious…doesn't always succeed. 40s/50s, Male.

SAMANTHA RILEY – Junior at Deans College. Super smart, grade obsessed, neurotically ambitious. Like Milo, her emotional development has taken a backseat to her other pursuits. Early 20s, Female.

JOEY GIAMANI – A Campus Security guard at Deans College. Milo's friend and protector. His toughness masks his vulnerability. 30s, Male.

GINA GIAMANI – Owner of the Blind Eagle—a local dive bar where the sports-obsessed working class and the scene-obsessed Deans College kids interact. Joey's sister. She's tough, like Joey, but way more in touch with her feelings. 30s, Female.

TITO DAVIS – Bouncer at the Blind Eagle. Brighter than he lets on. Very conniving, very enthusiastic, and, more often than not, very stoned. 30s/40s, Male.

SETTING

The area in and surrounding Deans College, in Dutchess County (upstate New York). To be more specific, the Tivoli, Red Hook, and Rhinebeck area.

TIME

November – March.

ACT 1

Scene 1

(The office of **G.H. HULIE** *– professor of psychology at Deans College in upstate New York.* **JOEY GIAMANI**, *a tough looking guy in a parka stands staring at the famous "Old Woman/Young Woman" optical illusion on the wall. He scratches himself. He squints harder at it. The door bursts open as* **HULIE** *enters.* **SAMANTHA** *follows holding a test.)*

HULIE. I'm not asking about *children* – I'm asking what did Freud say about four-year-old girls.

SAMANTHA. That they're 'polymorphously perverse.'

HULIE. No.

SAMANTHA. Yes! Yes he did!

HULIE. No, Freud said *all* humans are 'polymorphously perverse.' What I'm asking is what did he say about four-year-old girls.

SAMANTHA. That their libido starts to be discharged through the genitals.

HULIE. The genitals, correct. And which genital in particular.

SAMANTHA. The clitoris.

HULIE. The clitoris, correct. And where does Freud say the sexual focus *shifts* as the female reaches – key phrase here – "sexual maturity," hmm?

SAMANTHA. The um, y'know the –

HULIE. The vagina, correct. So if your test asks, "which stage of psychosexual development might Feminists take issue with?" the correct answer is The Phallic Stage due to the fact that any woman who continues to have orgasms from clitoral stimulation could be said to have, in Freud's eyes, the sexual maturity of a four-year-old girl. *(To* **JOEY.***)* Who are you.

JOEY. Joey Giamani. You the shrink?

SAMANTHA. But it's *not* The Phallic Stage – it's The Anal Stage!

HULIE. It's not the Anal Stage. I wrote an entire book on the Anal Stage called *The Anal Stage* and trust me, it's not the Anal Stage. *(To* **JOEY.***)* I'm sorry who are you?

JOEY. Joey Giamani. You the shrink?

HULIE. No, I'm G.H. Hulie, head of psychology here at Deans College.

JOEY. Yeah that's what I meant. Hulie.

SAMANTHA. But look, what you wrote on the test is "which stage of psychosexual development *might* Feminists take issue with." Well they *might* take issue with any number of stages!

HULIE. Samantha your grade stays the same. *(To* **JOEY.***)* I'm sorry, *what* did you want?

JOEY. I gotta talk to you about my buddy. He's all fucked up.

HULIE. I beg your pardon?

SAMANTHA. Look, in the Anal Stage the female is said to have a greater tendency –

HULIE. Samantha, are you serious? –

SAMANTHA. – a greater tendency to feel pleasure in the act of controlling the bowels – but that's like, *undeniably* sexist!

HULIE. Good, you're a very smart girl, with a very bright future, that I'm sure has many wonderful things in store for you, *but your grade stays the same.*

JOEY. So Doc, you gonna talk to my buddy or what? 'Cause I don't wanna tell him he got dragged all the way here for nothing.

(*The toilet flushes.*)

HULIE. Is someone using my bathroom?

JOEY. Yeah that's my buddy Milo. He's got an upset stomach. (*Lowers his voice.*) See, his mom passed away about a month ago, and it's only made things worse. I'm telling you he's got this really crazy thing going on that you never seen before. So you'll talk to him right?

HULIE. I'm sorry, *who* are you?

JOEY. Christ Doc – it's Joey Giamani! How many times I gotta say it!

> (**MILO MAZOWSKI**, *a tall, thin man child comes out of the bathroom wearing a parka that matches* **JOEY***'s and reading an enormous Psychology textbook that he presumably took from one of the shelves.*)

MILO. (*His head in the book.*) Hey Joey, you ever heard of this word: "polymorphous."

JOEY. See Doc, he looks like a regular guy, but I'm telling you he's got this really crazy thing going on!

HULIE. Sir, I'm not sure how you got in here –

JOEY. The broad outside. What's her face.

MILO. Ida.

JOEY. Yeah Ida. Your secretary or whatever. She let us in.

HULIE. Well she's supposed to have you wait outside.

(**SAMANTHA** *grabs the book from* **MILO***.*)

SAMANTHA. Can I see that for a sec? See it's right here in "Three Essays on the Theory of Sexuality!"

HULIE. Samantha *enough.*

SAMANTHA. Okay but just look at it for a second!

(*She shows him the book.*)

MILO. Who's she?

JOEY. Not important. Doc?

HULIE. All right, I see what you're referring to, it's a valid point, and we'll discuss it later okay?

SAMANTHA. And you might change my grade right?

(*The* **INTERCOM** *buzzes.*)

INTERCOM. Professor?

HULIE. Good Lord! (*To the* **INTERCOM**.) What is it Ida?

INTERCOM. I forgot to mention, there are two men waiting for you in your office.

HULIE. Yes I see that. You're supposed to have them wait outside, Ida.

INTERCOM. I know sir and I apologize. But that tall one's got a really crazy thing going on.

JOEY. See, I told you Doc.

HULIE. Sir – if you and your "*buddy*" would like to inquire about my services, you can schedule an appointment with my secretary.

MILO. You mean with Ida.

HULIE. Yes with Ida. But right now I need everyone in this room to kindly get out because I am expecting a very important phone call from my editor in…less than five minutes.

SAMANTHA. But the deadline for the Rosenhaas Fellowship is in two weeks!

HULIE. Well the deadline for my book proposal is today, so I win.

JOEY. No kidding, you writing a new book, Doc? What about.

HULIE. Gentlemen, I won't say it again. Please leave or I'll call Campus Security.

JOEY. Oh – we are Campus Security.

(**JOEY** *unzips his jacket revealing a campus security uniform.* **MILO** *does the same.*)

Thing is, we mostly work the weekends. And they just asked Milo not to come in this weekend.

MILO. Yeah I got "laid off." Whatever that means.

JOEY. It means you're fired, dipshit. See that's why we came to you, Doc. You gotta help him with his crazy thing, 'cause it's ruining his fucking life! Pardon me, sweetheart.

SAMANTHA. Dr. Hulie will you just at least consider changing it from an A- to an A.

HULIE. Samantha I'm about to change it from an A- to a B-.

SAMANTHA. No, please! It's just that I need a four-oh for the Rosenhaas Fellowship and if I get another A- it drops me down to a three-nine and I can't apply!

HULIE. Then you can't apply now SHUT UP AND LEAVE!

*(***SAMANTHA****'s face contorts and she starts crying.)*

JOEY. Well you didn't have to yell at her, Doc.

HULIE. All right Samantha please, I didn't mean to – please don't cry. I'm sorry. I've been stressed for personal reasons and – and I took it out on you.

SAMANTHA. *(Crying.)* You were short with me.

HULIE. I *was* short with you. I was. I shouldn't have been so…short.

SAMANTHA. *(Through tears.)* It's just that my parents met doing the Rosenhaas Fellowship and then my Dad died and it's like every time my Mom talks about him, she's like "You should have seen him when he did the Rosenhaas Fellowship, he wasn't even *bald* yet" and it's like this *thing* in my family, they even talk about Norman Rosenhaas who it's named after and who's like still alive even though he's 90 and senile and drools but he like told my mom at some fundraiser that I should apply, and so I've been working *really* hard –

HULIE. I know you have, you're a *very* good student.

SAMANTHA. I'm your *best* student! Except for Bushra, but she's like a genius.

HULIE. All right, well why don't we discuss this first thing Monday morning okay?

SAMANTHA. *(Fighting through tears.)* It's just…

HULIE. Yes?

SAMANTHA. It's just that… *(She wipes away the tears.)* It's just that Freud said in Three Essays on the Theory of Sexuality and I quote: "perverted feelings in females during The Anal Stage have increased the number of persons who can be added to the list of perverts."

HULIE. All right give me the goddamn test.

SAMANTHA. Thank you Dr. Hulie! Thank you *so* much!

MILO. Hey wait a minute, that's…no that's not right.

(They all look at **MILO.***)*

SAMANTHA. Uh, I think I would know what Freud said about Female Sexuality better than you would.

MILO. Mmmm, I don't know – I was just reading that book.

SAMANTHA. Yeah you mean in Dr. Hulie's bathroom? It says it Dr. Hulie you can check.

MILO. Mmmm, say it again?

SAMANTHA. What?

MILO. Say what you just said? I wanna double check.

SAMANTHA. Dr. Hulie, weren't you gonna like, escort these guys out?

HULIE. Actually I wasn't really paying close attention. Would you mind repeating it?

SAMANTHA. *(Scoffs.)* What, word for word?

MILO. Well yeah, how else?

SAMANTHA. *(Glaring at* **MILO.***)* Fine. What Freud says in Three Essays on the Theory of Sexuality, is "females have perverted feelings during The Anal Stage, which increases the number of persons who can be called perverts." Okay?

MILO. Well no, 'cause you just changed a couple of words from what you said before and also that's definitely not what it said.

SAMANTHA. Okay then smart guy – what did it say.

MILO. Well the part that I *think* you're talking about on page 225 said, "By demonstrating the perverted feelings as symptomatic formations in psycho-neurotics, we have enormously increased the number of persons who can be added to the perverts. This is not only because neurotics represent a very large proportion of humanity, but we must consider also that neuroses in all their gradations run in an uninterrupted series to the normal state." So yeah, it doesn't mention the word "female" there, but it does on page 223 and then on 230, and it doesn't mention the words "anal stage" in the essay at all actually – not until later in the book, on page 292. So I guess you were quoting from another essay in a different book that I didn't read? But I don't know, 'cause the truth is I read it kind of quickly and also I'm pretty hungry and when my stomach starts rumbling I get this green, hazy feeling in my eyes, so some of the passages were a little blurry, but if you want I think I could tell you what the rest of it said.

> *(The phone rings. And rings. **HULIE** stands dumbstruck.)*

HULIE. Are you saying you can recite verbatim the entire rest of that essay?

MILO. Well actually I meant the rest of the book. But I guess that might take awhile, huh?

JOEY. So Doc, you gonna help my buddy out or what?

> *(Lights out.)*

Scene 2

(The Blind Eagle – a dive bar in Tivoli, NY right near Deans College. **GINA**, *the owner, leans on the counter on a portable telephone. She looks like she's been there for a while.)*

GINA. No, I appreciate that Officer. And really, sincerely, it will never happen again – I *guarantee* you. *(Beat.)* What *else* can I guarantee you? *(She chuckles.)* Okay how about 10 percent on the weekends. Well 20's a little high sweetheart – how's 15? C'mon Officer, it's my birthday. No I'm *not* shitting you – November 15th. You're not supposed to ask a woman that! *(Beat.)* Thirty-five. Yup. Halfway through thirty. Is that so? Well I guess me and your daughter have the same birthday then. The birthstone? Oh uh, Topaz I think. *(Beat.)* T-O-P-A-Z, Topaz. Yeah, not that I got any…tell you what: how's 15 percent for Friday, Saturday and 20 for Thursday.

*(**TITO**, the bouncer saunters in, carrying a gym bag.)*

TITO. Wassup?

*(He sits at one of the stools and offers **GINA** a fist-pound. She ignores him.)*

GINA. *(On phone.)* Course, honey – obviously. We'll take real good care of you anytime you're in here. *And* your friends, okay? Okay you too Officer. Buh bye.

*(She hangs up. **TITO**'s fist is still out.)*

TITO. Yo, you leaving me hanging. *(She hits his hand with the phone.)* OW! What's that for? You *know* I got sensitive paws.

GINA. That was just the cops Tito.

TITO. The cops? What'd they want?

GINA. Oh, just to shut down this bar and arrest everyone who works here.

TITO. What for? Yo, I told you, I ain't dealing in here no more.

GINA. For serving alcohol to underage college kids – which apparently is what I did last night.

TITO. Well what'd you do that for? *(She slaps him upside the head.)* Ow!

GINA. 'Cause you let them in here you jackass! What'd I tell you about checking ID's, huh?

TITO. I do check 'em! It's just everyone's got fakes these days.

GINA. So you check 'em against the book Tito. If it's not in the book, you know it's a fake. You didn't even have the book last night!

TITO. Well I didn't want to scare them.

GINA. Yes, you *do* want to scare them! That's the whole point! You want to scare them so they don't try to give you a fake ID.

TITO. Nah but see if I scare them, I can't catch them in the act when they give me a fake one.

GINA. And how are you gonna know if it's a fake one or not?

TITO. 'Cause I'll check it against the book.

> **(GINA** *just looks at him. He snaps his fingers realizing the error of his logic.)*

See – that's the problem with that book.

GINA. No that's the problem with your brain! Give me one good reason why I shouldn't fire you right now?

TITO. 'Cause we're sleeping together?

GINA. *(Glares at him.)* Get out.

TITO. What, what'd I say?

GINA. Get out you're fired.

TITO. C'mon, I thought you were my girl.

GINA. Well I'm not. I'm your boss. And I'm not even that anymore.

TITO. Gina please – I need this job. Yo, my mom's in the hospital.

GINA. Oh, don't bring that up!

TITO. What, it's true! Look I screwed up okay? But when else have I ever screwed up like this?

GINA. Well let's see – couple months back, you broke that kid's wrist.

TITO. Yeah 'cause he was high on Ecstasy.

GINA. Which you sold to him.

TITO. Not in here I didn't.

GINA. You know what? I should've done this a long time ago. And you had to screw up today of all days!

TITO. Why what's today?

GINA. *(Imitating him.)* "Oh I thought you were my girl."

TITO. *(Not getting it.)* What?

GINA. Here get your shit out of here.

(She picks up his gym bag.)

TITO. Yo don't touch that!

GINA. *(Suspiciously.)* Are there drugs in here?

TITO. What? No!

GINA. Jesus Tito, there are! I can feel 'em – I can feel the little dime baggies in here!

TITO. Nah that's just – c'mon give it back.

(She unzips the bag.)

GINA. You lying little…

(She pulls out a jewelry case. She opens it up, revealing a necklace with gemstones.)

(Beat.) Are these um…

TITO. They're your birthstone. Topazes.

GINA. *(Gently correcting.)* Topaz.

TITO. Topaz.

GINA. How'd you afford this?

TITO. Don't worry about it. Not from selling drugs if that's what you're thinking! *(Beat.)* And yo, I got you some flowers too.

(**GINA** *pulls out some crumbled flowers.*)

GINA. *(Gently.)* Tito, you can't keep flowers in a gym bag.

TITO. *(Chuckling.)* I didn't wanna ruin the surprise.

GINA. Didn't want me to "catch you in the act," huh?

TITO. That's right.

GINA. Aw Tito, now I'm supposed to kick back 15 percent to the cops like every night.

TITO. So take it out of my wages. And let me take you to dinner tomorrow. Someplace fancy.

GINA. What about your mom.

TITO. Nah, let's just keep it you and me.

(**GINA** *smiles despite herself.*)

GINA. You're cute, but you're dumb.

TITO. I'm cute *'cause* I'm dumb.

GINA. *Really* dumb.

TITO. Ignorance is bliss baby.

GINA. C'mere stupid.

(They kiss. And start making out. **MILO** *enters carrying a bouquet of flowers. He sees them and freezes awkwardly. He turns right around and bumps into* **JOEY** *entering.)*

JOEY. Where you going. *(Sees them making out.)* Hey c'mon, knock it off!

(**GINA** *stops embarrassed at being caught.*)

TITO. Hey what up, Joey.

JOEY. My friends call me Joey. You can call me Joe. Happy birthday sis. Hey I got you a gift.

GINA. *(Excited.)* Oh yeah?

JOEY. Yeah, close your eyes, hold out your hands. (**JOEY** *licks his finger and puts it in her ear.)* Wet willy!

GINA. Aw c'mon! *(Wiping her ear.)* Ugh, you always use way too much spit.

JOEY. That's what she said.

(They laugh.)

GINA. Shut up!

JOEY. Nah, I'm just kidding. Your day off's tomorrow right? I'm taking you out to dinner.

GINA. Oh um, Tito's actually taking me to dinner tomorrow.

TITO. *(Nodding.)* Wassup.

JOEY. Where you taking her.

GINA.	TITO.
Oh we didn't decide yet.	Chipotle. *(Beat.)* Nah, I mean, we didn't decide yet.

JOEY. Well when you figure it out, let me know. But right now we're all taking shots.

GINA. No, Joey, I gotta open.

JOEY. Don't care. It's your birthday. And also we got a celebratory announcement. Right Milo?

GINA. Oh hey Milo! I didn't even see you there.

MILO. *(Chuckling.)* Yeah – you usually say that even though I'm really tall.

GINA. *(Baby voice.)* I know, so tall and handsome.

(GINA points to the flowers MILO holds.)

Hey, those for me?

MILO. Hmm? Oh yeah since today is November 15th, which is your birthday, I got these for you for your birthday.

GINA. Well thank you, that's very sweet of you. *(She smells them.)* Mmm, Chrysanthemums. Just like *you* got me Tito.

TITO. Huh? Oh yeah right, Chry uh, yeah.

(JOEY finishes pouring the shots.)

MILO. Yeah my day planner said it's the flower of November so that's why I got it for you. And I got you something else that my day planner suggested too –

JOEY. Milo shut up. Everyone grab a shot. A year older but still does yoga. And to my good buddy Milo. Milo – tell 'em the celebratory announcement.

MILO. Right, well, I got "laid off" today, which means I got fired.

JOEY. Not that. The other thing. Y'know – afterwards?

MILO. Hmm? Oh yeah, then I went to see a shrink.

JOEY. *(Sighs.)* And what did the shrink say.

MILO. That he's going to write a book about me.

GINA. Wait, what?

JOEY. That's right. I brought Milo in to talk to that shrink guy over at Deans? They ended up chit-chatting for like two hours. Then he says he wants to do a 'case-study' on Milo 'cause of his trick and help him be more normal.

TITO. What trick?

MILO. It's pretty easy. You say stuff to me and I say stuff back to you.

TITO. That ain't a trick. That's called talking.

MILO. Yeah that's what I said, but Joey said no it's a trick. And this shrink guy agreed with him.

GINA. He can remember anything Tito.

TITO. What do you mean anything?

GINA. Like *anything.*

JOEY. *(To* **TITO**.*)* What's the longest thing you have memorized.

TITO. *(Laughing.)* What? I don't know man. A poem I had to recite in grade school.

JOEY. Oh yeah? Go ahead and recite it.

TITO. *(Snorts.)* Fine. "The Angel that presided o'er my birth. Said 'Little Creature, formed of Joy and Mirth. Go love without the help of anything on earth.'"

GINA. That's beautiful. Who is that?

TITO. That right there is some William Blake.

(GINA nods, impressed.)

JOEY. Milo. Recite it backwards.

MILO. *(Quickly.)* Earth on anything of help the without love go. Mirth and Joy of formed creature little said. Birth my o'er presided that angel the.

(**TITO** *stares at him awestruck.*)

TITO. Jesus, you're a fucking freak man!

JOEY. What'd you say?

TITO. Nah nah, I meant it as a complement. Y'know like a 'Super-Freak.' I'm just saying.

GINA. Do you know any other poems Milo?

MILO. Well right now I mostly know the 'Campus Security Safety And Awareness Handbook.' But if you give me a book of poems, I would be really excited to learn them for you.

TITO. Yeah, but do you know what they mean?

MILO. Hmm?

TITO. I mean like the metaphors and stuff. You know what the symbolism means and all that?

JOEY. Who cares? Can *you* recite an entire book right after reading it?

TITO. Well what good's reciting it, if you don't know what any of it means?

JOEY. He knows what it means!

TITO. Okay, so "The Angel that presided o'er my birth" – what's that mean?

JOEY. *(Softly.)* 'O'er' means 'over' Milo.

TITO. Yo, don't help him!

(*There's a knock in the back.*)

GINA. Shit, that's my beer delivery. Joey broey, give me a hand.

JOEY. Me? *(Points to* **TITO.***)* Why not him?

GINA. *(Baby voice.)* 'Cause you're so strong. *(To* **TITO.***)* And 'cause you gotta check ID's, right?

(**TITO** *grabs the book and holds it up.* **JOEY** *exits out the back.*)

Hey, I wanna hear more about this book deal Mr. Milo, so don't go anywhere.

(**MILO** *sees the necklace in her hand.*)

MILO. Hey, what's that.

GINA. What this? It's a birthday gift from Tito.

(**GINA** *exits out the back.* **MILO** *sits there thinking.*)

TITO. So hey – you say you got fired?

MILO. Yeah, "laid off."

(**TITO** *pours himself a shot.*)

TITO. Shit that sucks. What for?

MILO. Mmm, not really sure. We had our weekly meeting today and Ken Lugar our boss started listing all the noise complaints made on campus in the past week and he said that we "weren't working hard enough 'cause Thanksgiving was coming up" and he saw that I wasn't taking notes and he got really angry and he said "how come you're not writing any of this down Milo" and I said "I never write anything you say down, I don't know why other people do" and he said that this was "the straw that broke the camel's back" with me, and Joey tried to reason with him, but he told me not to come in anymore.

TITO. Damn. So what you gonna do now?

MILO. Yeah it's a good question. I really need money. I got some when my mom died last month. But I was hoping to save it. So Joey says that when I see this shrink guy for our first "session" next week, I should talk to him about *(Air quotes.)* "compensation."

TITO. Yeah man, don't let this guy make a quick buck off you. Shit's expensive these days.

MILO. Yeah. *(Thinks for a moment.)* Hmm, that's odd.

TITO. What.

MILO. Well Gina's necklace present from you had sixteen pieces of Topaz on it.

TITO. Pretty nice, right? *(Conspiratorially.)* Yo, you wanna know where I got it?

MILO. Sure but it's just odd because my day planner said Topaz was the birthstone for November so I bought her a necklace that also had sixteen pieces of Topaz on it and went to her house this morning to give it to her before work, but nobody answered and through the window it looked like she was still asleep, even though I could see someone was making a fruit smoothie in her kitchen while running in place with headphones on, like they were about to go jogging, so I just left the jewelry case by the door with a couple of those flowers I got alongside it, 'cause I didn't want to wake her, and I figured she'd see it when she opened the door, but I was really tired at the time so my eyes were all green and tingly and maybe I even left it at the wrong house. So where'd you get yours from?

TITO. Uh, jewelry store. Yup. *(Beat.)*

(**MILO** *nods, still thinking. Lights out.*)

Scene 3

> (*HULIE's office.* **SAMANTHA** *sits using* **HULIE**'s *computer. She keeps looking up as if afraid someone might walk in. She hears a noise.*)

SAMANTHA. Hello? (*She waits.*) Dr. Hulie?

> (*She waits a moment then resumes typing.* **MILO** *comes out of the bathroom.*)

MILO. Hi there.

SAMANTHA. Ah! Jesus, you almost gave me a heart attack. Have you been in there this whole time?

MILO. Yeah. Where's Dr. Hulie?

SAMANTHA. He's coming, he's in a psych department meeting. (*Quietly to herself.*) Probably discussing the orgasms of four-year-old girls.

MILO. He discusses things like that?

SAMANTHA. What? Yes it arouses him.

> (**MILO** *stares at her.*)

I'm being sarcastic. Forget it, he'll be here soon.

MILO. Oh great. Hey, y'know who wasn't out by her desk? Ida.

SAMANTHA. Yeah, she's out to lunch.

MILO. Oh right. My lunch didn't "sit well" with me.

SAMANTHA. That's great. So Dr. Hulie picked me as his research assistant for this whole book project thing, so that's why I'm here in case you're wondering. I'll be here like every session.

MILO. Oh great. Were you writing an essay about "Freud" just now?

SAMANTHA. What? No, I was just writing an email.

> (**MILO** *nods. Awkward silence.*)

MILO. Did you see the sun today?

SAMANTHA. Did I see the sun? Yes I *did* the see the sun today.

MILO. It was particularly juicy this morning, don't you think? Even though it's almost Thanksgiving.

(**SAMANTHA** *starts texting.*)

Looks like you're texting someone.

SAMANTHA. Uh I am, I'm texting my mom.

MILO. Ah, the one who met your dad doing the Rosenhaas Fellowship. Oh did you get into that?

SAMANTHA. Uh nope, I wasn't able to apply, remember?

(*She keeps texting.*)

MILO. Oh right 'cause of what I said. (*Clears his throat.*) Are you texting her about Thanksgiving?

SAMANTHA. Uh, nope.

MILO. Are you texting her about the sun?

SAMANTHA. No, I'm not.

MILO. Are you texting her about –

(**HULIE** *enters, happily.*)

HULIE. Ah hello there. Sorry to keep you guys waiting – I couldn't get off this conference call with my editor and my publisher. It appears there's a lot of buzz about this book already. Let's just say it could be the basis for something bigger.

SAMANTHA. Whoa – like a movie about his life?

HULIE. (*Coyly.*) Or perhaps a segment on *This American Life.* Sorry. Temper expectations. Milo, good to see you. You remember Samantha. She'll be joining us as my assistant.

MILO. "That's what she said!" (*He chuckles.*) It's a joke. My friend Joey says it a lot. It usually makes people laugh.

SAMANTHA. Right, except that is literally what I said.

MILO. Yeah exactly.

HULIE. (*Clears his throat.*) So how was your weekend Milo?

MILO. Pretty good. It was my favorite friend Gina's birthday. She runs that bar The Blind Eagle in Tivoli.

>(**HULIE** *takes of his sweater. He's wearing a very colorful tie.*)

HULIE. Ah, fantastic. And do you have any plans for Thanksgiving? Family coming in?

MILO. *(Squinting.)* Mmm, no, my mom…my mom just died, so…that's a, that's a loud tie.

HULIE. What's that?

MILO. Your tie. It's really loud.

HULIE. Oh, uh, yes it was an anniversary gift from my wife. Some gift, huh?

>(**MILO** *puts his hands over his ears.*)

Are you all right?

MILO. It's just a little too loud for me. *(Loudly.)* CAN YOU TAKE IT OFF?

HULIE. *(Confused.)* Uhhhh…sure…

>(**HULIE** *starts taking the tie off.*)

SAMANTHA. Hey wait a minute, maybe he's a seh-nes, um, sehnes-themo?

HULIE. A synesthete?

SAMANTHA. Yeah a synesthete! I mean that would explain why he can remember stuff so well, right?

HULIE. Yes, yes it would. That's – why didn't *I* think of that?

SAMANTHA. Well I only thought of it 'cause of that lecture you gave.

HULIE. That's true, teamwork.

MILO. Wait, I'm a what?

HULIE. Your reaction to my tie Milo, and the way things make you, uh, see colors – those are symptoms of a condition called "*Synesthesia.*"

MILO. That's a funny looking word.

HULIE. Yes exactly! You *see* it don't you? The word I mean.

MILO. Well yeah, you can't really miss it with its slimy face and prickly smile: "*Synesthesia.*"

HULIE. Right well Synesthesia is where one sensation sort of *spills* over into another. So you literally hear smells. Taste images. Even have physical reactions to strong emotions. *Itchiness* for instance is often linked with feeling awkward or uncomfortable.

MILO. *(Chuckling.)* Really? Itchiness. That's weird.

HULIE. *(Chuckles.)* Yes, well, I'm no neurologist but…the *strength* of your synesthesia coupled with the *speed* at which your brain intuits information – it would almost suggest that your sense memory has no limits. I mean… you could literally be unable to forget. Sorry, I know this is a lot to take in. Does this make sense?

MILO. Yeah. Itchiness. Unable to forget. Got it. Can I ask a quick question though?

HULIE. Of course.

MILO. It's a little *(Air quote.)* "awkward."

HULIE. That's okay.

MILO. How much money do I get for all this?

HULIE. *(Beat.)* Beg your pardon?

              (MILO *starts scratching himself.)*

MILO. *(Scratching.)* Well my friend Joey, who you met, said since you're a pretty well-known guy, you must get a pretty big 'advance,' whatever that means, and so, wow it's itchy in here, I thought I should ask you: How much money do I get?

HULIE. Ah. Yes. Well, uh… *(Chuckles.)* Now I'm itchy too.

MILO. *(Chuckling.)* We're both so itchy!

              (They chuckle awkwardly.)

SAMANTHA. Um, should I leave?

HULIE. No, no, that's all right. Uh, look Milo: what people usually do when I offer them my services, that is to say when I analyze their psychological makeup and give my expertise, is *they* pay *me*. This along with teaching and book writing is how I earn my livelihood. Now obviously you're a special case. So special in fact that in exchange for allowing me to write a case-study on you, I'm willing to waive my fee to analyze *your* makeup.

MILO. But I'm not wearing any makeup.

HULIE. Makeup can also mean "composition" or "structure" Milo.

MILO. How can one word mean three different things?

HULIE. We'll get to that. But first, let me ask you a question: have you ever felt left out of a conversation? Or been unable to make new friends and unsure why? Heard people laughing about something, but you can't quite figure out why it's so funny?

MILO. Yeah that last one happens a lot actually.

HULIE. Well, what I'm prepared to do Milo, is help you figure out why these people are laughing and how to become more socially comfortable, so that you can make new friends. And have better relationships with the ones you *do* have like, uh, Joey or –

MILO. *(Perks up.)* Or Gina?

HULIE. Well, yes or your friend Gina for that matter.

MILO. Mmm…so you're saying no money. But you'll teach me how to make Gina laugh.

HULIE. Well it's not a joke class per se, but how to be in a better position to understand why she laughs and relate to her more, yes.

MILO. Hmmm. *(He thinks for a moment.)* Okay it's a deal.

HULIE. Okay. Wonderful. Well, Ida will draw up some papers for you to sign. But while you're here, let's get started.

MILO. Okay.

HULIE. What I want to do is have you memorize something – and just have you tell me which color the thing I read to you makes you feel, all right? Samantha, what's on my bookshelf?

SAMANTHA. *(Looking.)* Let's see… Ericksson, Jung…a cookbook…a book of poetry –

MILO. *(Perks up.)* Poetry. I'll take the poetry book.

HULIE. *(Sees the book.)* Ah yes. Some wonderful compositions in here.

MILO. *(With a sly grin.)* You mean some wonderful *"make up."*

(**MILO** *looks to* **HULIE** *for approval.)*

HULIE. Not quite. But we'll get there.

(Lights out.)

Scene 4

(The Blind Eagle. Thanksgiving night. A couple of tacky Turkey decorations are up. **TITO** *stands behind the bar, eating Chipotle, watching TV.)*

TITO. Tackle him. Tackle him. *Tackle HIM!*

(Nobody gets tackled. **JOEY** *walks in wearing his campus security uniform.* **TITO** *quickly grabs the remote and changes the channel.)*

Joey – what up.

JOEY. *(Warming his hands up.)* Hey. Gettin' cold out.

TITO. Word. Yo, you worked today?

JOEY. Yeah can you believe that shit? Not a single person's on campus. Anyway Merry Thanksgiving or what have you. Where's Gina?

TITO. In the back with some peeps.

JOEY. Huh?

TITO. Peeps. People. High rollers actually – bought a shit ton of rounds.

JOEY. Oh yeah? Guess a little holiday business never hurt anyone. What are you watching?

TITO. Oh uh, *(He looks.)* QVC – the home shopping channel. Y'know it was already on, so.

JOEY. Oh well put the game on.

TITO. *(Lying.)* Nah, I'm kinda into this.

JOEY. You just said you weren't even watching. Put the game on.

*(***TITO*** picks up the remote and changes it to the game.* **JOEY** *looks at the score.)*

Yeah, baby! Boom! Y'know I got big money riding on this game. *(***TITO*** starts to move away discreetly.)* Hey wait a minute. I got money on this game with *you.*

TITO. Huh? With me?

JOEY. Yeah what the fuck am I saying? *You're* the one I bet on this game with.

TITO. Nah, we talked about it, but I don't think we bet.

JOEY. Aw shut the fuck up – it was two hundred bucks to the winner!

TITO. Nah, it was two hundred bucks for the *spread*.

JOEY. Oh so *now* you remember! Well whatever – the spread was a touchdown.

TITO. You sure? I thought it was two touchdowns.

*(**MILO** comes in from the back room.)*

JOEY. Hey Milo – you were here last Friday, right buddy?

TITO. Yo, don't bring him into this.

JOEY. Did I or did I not make a bet with Tito.

MILO. Mmm, yes Tito said "Detroit's defensive line can stop a truck" and you said "Not a truck named the Texans" and Tito said, "care to make a wager?" and you said, "you're on."

JOEY. And did we or did we not say the spread would be a touchdown.

TITO. Aw c'mon, now you're just influencing him.

JOEY. He's a human computer, he doesn't get influenced. What'd we say the spread was?

MILO. *(Quietly.)* I'm not a human computer.

JOEY. Huh?

MILO. I said I'm not a human computer. I'm a human being with human emotions.

JOEY. Yeah, I know buddy. Y'know it's just a figure of speech. It means like "genius."

MILO. Oh. Well I'm having a hard time with these "figures of speech" things. Anyway, you said "I'll give you a two touchdown spread –

TITO. See!

MILO. And then Tito said "I don't need no charity, make it one –

TITO. What?! That didn't happen!

MILO. And then you said, "one it is" and you two shook hands.

TITO. Yeah well it ain't over til it's over.

> *(They stare at the TV for about ten seconds.)*

JOEY. And it's over. Two hundred big ones baby.

TITO. Yeah yeah.

> **(JOEY** *stares at* **TITO** *expectantly.)*

What, *now?*

JOEY. Well when else?

TITO. Yo I don't got it on me – when Gina's done with those peeps, she'll spot me.

MILO. Those what?

TITO. Peeps. People. What's wrong with y'all?

JOEY. I don't want my sister giving me money that *you* owe!

MILO. Here I have some money.

> **(MILO** *pulls a wad of hundred dollar bills.)*

JOEY. Jesus Milo, where'd you get all that?!

MILO. Mmm, back there. *(He points to the back room.)* From the peeps.

TITO. The high rollers gave you that?

MILO. Yeah they're from the City. They didn't believe I could remember things, so they kept making these bets with me and asking me trivia questions and I guess I kept winning.

TITO. You "*guess*" you kept winning? How much you got there?

MILO. Five hundred bucks. Oh no wait. Six hundred. Anyway, here's some money Tito.

JOEY. Whoa – you're not giving him shit Milo. And also what'd I tell you about that stuff?

MILO. What stuff? Trivia?

JOEY. Spouting stuff for people. *(Points to his head.)* Indulging that part of your what-have-you.

MILO. But you just asked me to remember what your bet was.

JOEY. It's different – you weren't performing for me like some monkey! I thought that shrink guy was trying to help you be more normal.

MILO. He *is* trying. I'm trying.

JOEY. All right, well try a little harder then! Look buddy, it's just… I don't like it when people treat you like a freak, y'know? So uh what kind of questions they ask you back there.

MILO. Mmm, sports questions mostly. They're big Knicks fans.

JOEY. Oh yeah? Well shit, I wanna see what these High Rollers know. Maybe I can win some dough too. How drunk are they?

MILO. *(Chuckles.)* Pretty drunk. One guy meant to hand me a ten, but he handed me a hundred.

JOEY. *(To* TITO.*)* Y'know I stumped this guy once right? Go on, tell him Milo.

MILO. *(Giggles.)* Yeah.

TITO. Bullshit. What'd he get you with?

JOEY. Who's the only pitcher in major league history who won over 300 games, had over 2,000 strikeouts, a career ERA under three, and never *once* won a CY Young Award?

TITO. *(Thinks for a minute.)* I give up. Who.

JOEY. Cy Young. Boom!

> *(**JOEY** exits to the back.)*

TITO. *(Quietly.)* Asshole.

> *(**MILO** looks at him.)*

Nah, I mean…so hey how's the job hunt going?

MILO. Mmm, not very good. I applied to that Chinese restaurant Millhouse Panda in Rhinebeck? But the music there is awful.

TITO. What do you mean? The Chinese music?

MILO. Yeah, it makes everything taste like soap. I told them they should just play the oldies station 'cause oldies make everything taste good, but that made them upset. Also all the menus are filthy, which makes the food taste dirty. I don't know how people eat there.

TITO. *(Beat.)* So no job yet.

MILO. Nope. I wish I could just answer trivia for a living.

TITO. Yeah right. *(Beat.)* Yo, that's not a bad idea actually.

MILO. Hmm?

TITO. *(Thinking.)* Holy shit. Yo, wait a minute. We could do that.

MILO. Do what.

TITO. Fucking make a show out of it. You answering trivia, doing math problems *(He snaps his fingers.)* memorizing and reciting entire passages from like famous books and movies, doing memory tricks – that kind of thing.

MILO. You mean like performing for people?

TITO. Yeah man – we could go around this entire area. Do a whole fucking college tour!

MILO. Are you stoned?

TITO. No! *(Beat.)* I mean yes a little, but yo I'm serious about this! Think about it: a college like Deans? They got these fucking rich prep kids everywhere, looking for fun shit to do. I went to a show at the Campus Center like a month ago? It was a slam poetry show.

MILO. What's slam poetry?

TITO. It's like poetry but with people shouting.

MILO. That sounds awful.

TITO. Yo, when it's bad, it's *bad* – but they were charging 20 bucks a pop for that shit. And there's no reason why we can't do that too! Except we make it 25, *30* bucks a pop. Fill an auditorium that seats a hundred and fifty people? That's like uh… *(He thinks.)*

MILO. 3,750 or 4,500 dollars a show depending on if we charge 25 or 30.

TITO. That's what I'm saying! *(Beat.)* How'd you do that so fast?

MILO. Well twenty-five's a fluffy number, which if you think of it in cotton balls –

TITO. Y'know what, never mind. The point is, all we need? Is a mic and you. That's it.

MILO. Yeah, but I don't have a mic.

TITO. I got a mic.

MILO. Oh wow. But I get nervous when I'm put on the spot. And also what if Joey's right and doing this stuff makes me worse? 'Cause y'know Dr. Hulie said I might never be able to forget anything. What if my brain explodes? I don't know…

TITO. Milo you need a job right? Well what if I told you your job could be memorizing shit – the one thing you're good at! No offense. But even Joey showed your 'trick' off to me the first time we met. And I mean shit, you see the way Gina looked at you?

MILO. What? When? No. How?

TITO. When you recited that poem – she was in awe of you man! And yo, we're talking big bucks here. Not just at Deans. There's mad money in all those schools nearby. I'm talking Vassar, Marist, SUNY New Paltz, the fucking Culinary Institute of America son!

MILO. Wow, you know a lot of schools around here.

TITO. Well, a lot of those kids buy weed from me. Or y'know, used to. My point is, I know this whole area. And all we gotta do is promote the hell out of it at Deans first – then let word of mouth do the rest. Yo, I even know what we'll call it! We'll put up flyers all around campus that say: "Come And Try To Stump… The Meh-nemonist of Dutchess County!"

MILO. The what?

TITO. Oh "Meh-nemonist." That's the term for people like you. I googled it. It means like a guy with a limitless memory.

MILO. Hm. (Realizing.) Oh, you mean Mnemonist.

TITO. Nah, I'm pretty sure it's Meh-nemonist.

MILO. Oh. I guess Dr. Hulie's been saying it wrong then.

TITO. Tell you what: you let me worry about all the publicity and promotional stuff and meanwhile you just start memorizing shit. Trivial pursuit cards, Shakespeare plays, whatever. We do this right? We could have our first show before Christmas break.

MILO. Gina really looked at me in awe? 'Cause I do like the sound of that. And I *could* use a job.

TITO. Hey – two birds with one stone.

MILO. *(Nodding.)* Two birds and a stone!

TITO. That's right – so shake my hand partner! *(They shake hands.)* Sixty, forty.

MILO. Sixty, forty! *(Beat.)* What's sixty, forty?

TITO. The money we split. Sixty for me for organizing and forty for you.

MILO. Oh right. Is that standard?

TITO. Y'know. Basically. **(GINA** *enters.* **TITO** *sees her.)* But hey let's keep this on the down-low for now. Y'know, too many cooks in the kitchen sort of thing. *(To* **GINA.***)* Hey baby what's up. *(He kisses her on the cheek.)* Yo, you smell like wine.

GINA. *(Embarrassed.)* What? No I don't. Hey Milo.

MILO. Hey. Hi Gina.

TITO. I gotta take a mean piss, I'll be right back.

> **(TITO** *exits to the back.* **GINA** *goes behind the counter and starts adding up receipts.)*

MILO. So Tito says you hired some new cooks in the kitchen.

GINA. Uh…nope. No new cooks.

MILO. Huh. Wonder why he said that. *(Awkward silence.)* Hey, you wanna hear a joke?

GINA. Uh…sure.

> **(MILO** *clears his throat.)*

MILO. *(Quickly.)* So a piece of string walks into a bar and says "I'll have a beer please" but the bartender says "sorry pal, we don't serve string." So the string walks outside, sees a woman, and says, "excuse me miss, but would you fray my ends a little?" She goes sure, frays his ends, the string walks back inside, says "I'll have a beer please." The bartender says, "I just told you we don't serve string." So the string walks outside, sees a guy, says "excuse me sir, but would you tie me in a knot." The guy goes sure, ties him in a knot, the string comes back inside, says "I'll have a beer please." The bartender says "Hey aren't you that string?" And the string says "I'm a Frayed Knot."

(He looks at her. She smiles and nods.)

"I'm a Frayed Knot." If you spell it out it makes sense because –

GINA. No, no, I get it. It's funny.

MILO. Oh. Good. *(He starts scratching his arm.)* Well, merry thanksgiving or what have you...

GINA. Y'know I think that might be the first joke I've ever heard you tell.

MILO. *(Sitting back down.)* Well I know 4 more. Dr. Hulie taught them to me.

GINA. Who? Oh right, the book guy – I totally forgot. How's that going?

MILO. Pretty good. He's teaching me to be more "social."

GINA. *(Smiling.)* You *do* seem more social.

MILO. *(Proudly.)* Yeah.

GINA. God, I can't believe someone's writing a book about you. So when does it come out?

MILO. Oh I don't know. I guess he's gotta finish it first. Probably around springtime.

GINA. Oh no, that's so far. Well you'll have to send me a copy.

MILO. Yeah. *(Beat.)* But can't I just give you one?

GINA. Right. Well I don't want to jinx it, but um, it looks like I might be leaving or something.

MILO. Might be?

GINA. Am. Am leaving.

MILO. Oh. Like on vacation.

GINA. Um. Moving actually.

MILO. What? Why? Where?

GINA. Well it looks like there might be some people interested in buying the bar. Those guys back there from The City? We've been talking for a couple of weeks. Technically I'm not supposed to say anything yet – but they just walked right in here the other day and made me an offer. I mean I guess every other place around here near the Hudson is getting bought and refurbished. Anyway I just want to take my money and get out of this dump.

MILO. You don't like it here?

GINA. No it's just… I've been here too long, y'know? It's like you begin to notice things like how the only clear radio station plays the same 9 oldie songs over and over again and how the only people around here are either college kids or trust-fund hippies, or sports-obsessed meatheads. *(Beat.)* And I don't like the nights here, so…

MILO. The nights?

GINA. Um, no nevermind.

MILO. No, what do you mean.

GINA. Well it's like, growing up around here I was always scared of the wind at night, y'know? There's such a particular howl it has. And it used to remind me of like ghosts and werewolves and, I don't know, just horror movie stuff. But then as I grew up, it started reminding me of other things. Much scarier things. Like…growing old I guess. And being alone. Just totally completely alone where you go out during the day and shop for groceries just so you can eat them by yourself at night while you watch these TV shows that are filled with images of a world you don't even belong to. But that you convince yourself you *do*. And you keep trying to remember what it was like to be there, 'cause you can't face the fact that you're totally isolated. Alienated from everything and just completely alone. And you just keep on passing the time, passively passing time. Until you're old. And your bones won't move. And then that's it, there's nothing left. There's just – and you never even… *(She gets choked up. She takes a deep breath.)* Sorry.

Maybe I'm crazy. I just don't want to hear that howl anymore y'know? I wanna go someplace warm, where the sun sets late, and there are lots of people around and I don't have to drive all the time and I just never want to hear that howl again.

MILO. Here's a Chipotle napkin.

GINA. Thanks. Thank you. *(She dabs her eyes.)* Anyway, I gotta go meet the fam for Thanksgiving dinner at the Rhinecliff Motel.

MILO. Oh really? I don't like that place. It smells too much like oysters.

GINA. It does right! Like cheap oysters!

MILO. Yeah, it reminds me of that T.S. Eliot poem actually: "Let us go, through certain half-deserted streets. The muttering retreats. Of restless nights in one-night cheap hotels. And sawdust restaurants with oyster-shells."

GINA. *(Impressed.)* That's "The Song of J. Alfred Prufrock" right?

MILO. Actually it's called "The *Love* Song of J. Alfred Prufrock."

GINA. *(Smiles.)* Right. "I grow old, I grow old, I shall wear the bottoms of my trousers rolled."

MILO. Yeah that's right. Isn't it great? It's one of my favorite poems.

GINA. *(Smiles.)* Me too.

MILO. Really? Or are you just saying that 'cause I said it.

GINA. Shut up! *(She hits him playfully.)* Hey, I need a drink – you wanna have a drink with me?

MILO. *(Dismissively.)* Nah, that stuff's too red for me. *(It occurs to him what he just said.)* Whaaat? I mean, yes, let's have a drink.

GINA. You sure?

MILO. Yeah it's Thanksgiving! *(**GINA** pours two glasses. They drink.)* Whoa, that stuff's great! What is that?

GINA. Yeah, it's called Armagnac.

MILO. Well I *love* Armagnac!

    *(**GINA** laughs.)*

GINA. Hey what are you doing tonight anyway? I mean, I know this is the first Thanksgiving your mom's not around for.

MILO. Yeah, I was just gonna go home and memorize all the trivial pursuit cards.

    (She laughs, then sees he isn't joking.)

GINA. Uh…well do you want to come and have dinner with us instead?

MILO. Oh, I would but Joey said before that he was just gonna keep it family tonight.

GINA. Milo, at this point? You're practically family.

    (She gives him a big kiss on the cheek.)

MILO. Oh. Well great.

    *(**JOEY** comes out from the back.)*

JOEY. Hey, you ready to roll?

GINA. Yeah. So hey, Milo's gonna join us for some Turkey.

JOEY. Oh. I uh thought it was just gonna be family.

GINA. Well I already invited Tito.

JOEY. Tito?! Milo, you're coming.

GINA. Where *is* Tito? He's been in the bathroom forever.

JOEY. Yeah if by "in the bathroom" you mean "doing coke in the back with a couple of patrons," then yeah he's been doing that for a real long time.

GINA. Fuck 'im, let's leave.

(She exits to the kitchen. **JOEY** *stops* **MILO**.*)*

JOEY. Hey buddy – can I borrow a hundred bucks? Those assholes from the City know a lot of trivia.

(Lights out.)

Scene 5

(HULIE's office. HULIE, MILO, and SAMANTHA all look incredibly frustrated.)

MILO. But I got it right!

HULIE. Yes but the point I'm trying to make is that this exercise is not about the words themselves – it's about the meaning behind them! Let's take it again, but slower.

MILO. So I should say it again.

HULIE. Yes, but remember to pay close atten –

MILO. Yeah, yeah "pay close attention to the spacing of the lines" I know. "So much depends. Upon. A red wheel. Barrow. Glazed with rain. Water. Beside the white. Chickens."

HULIE. Good. Now what does this poem mean to you?

MILO. "So much depends –

HULIE. No, don't repeat the words. I want to know what comes to mind when you say them. When you think of a 'wheel barrow,' for instance, a 'wheel barrow' is –

MILO. *(Correcting.)* A *red* wheel barrow.

HULIE. Yes, well forget the color for a moment.

MILO. Forget the color?

HULIE. Yes, if you think of a 'wheel-barrow' – *(MILO starts writing something down.)* What are you doing.

MILO. You said "forget the color," so it's this new method I figured out. If I write something down and throw it away, I can forget it.

SAMANTHA. Really? That works?

MILO. Yeah, but usually I only do it for little grey gangly things that I don't want to store in any of my houses, like movie times and food orders, y'know small things like that.

SAMANTHA. Your what? Your *houses?*

HULIE. All right, Samantha, you'll be out of here soon enough. Let's get back to the poem.
Now when you hear the words 'wheel-barrow,' what do you picture?

MILO. Mmm, an old wooden wheel-barrow my mom used to make me carry as a kid before she died a couple months ago of pancreatic cancer.

HULIE. Ah. Right.

SAMANTHA. Whoa, really? That's what my Dad died of – pancreatic cancer.

MILO. *(Matter of factly.)* Yeah as far as cancers go it's pretty common.

HULIE. Well forgive me.

MILO. For what.

HULIE. No I mean *(He clears his throat.)* – sorry continue about the 'wheel-barrow.'

MILO. Well my mom used to take me to the Rhinebeck fairgrounds and make me carry an old wheel-barrow and I'd have to pose for a picture like I was living in ancient times.

HULIE. Okay – "ancient times." And do you know what people used it for in "ancient times"?

MILO. Yeah to carry things.

HULIE. Good! So when most people think of a wheel-barrow, they think of carrying things.

MILO. Do they?

HULIE. They do.

MILO. Oh okay. Carrying things.

HULIE. Yes, but does the poem talk about how the wheel-barrow carries things?

MILO. Mmm…no.

HULIE. Excellent. What does it talk about instead?

MILO. The… "glazed rain."

HULIE. Yes exactly! The imagery of the scene.

MILO. How it looks.

HULIE. Yes!

MILO. That's an interesting word – "glazed."

HULIE. Yes, "Glazed" – beautiful!

MILO. "Beside the white chickens." Chickens aren't usually *white*!

HULIE. Exactly! And yet it conjures the notion of "purity" and "simplicity" – do you see that?

MILO. Yeah, I can see it! And smell it, and hear it –

HULIE. Yes, the whole world around the wheel-barrow! You see? The poem is about the whole beautiful world around the objects we take for granted. About how even the most mundane, functional objects have an intrinsic beauty to them! Be it a 'wheel-barrow' or a 'chicken' – so much of life, of our drab work life, *depends* on us seeing these objects every day and yet the poem is realigning our perspective about them! It's saying we must not take them for granted – we must take note of their beauty as well – do you see?!

MILO. Yeah! *(Beat.)* Except it doesn't say that – what it says is "So much depends upon a wheel barrow glazed with rain water beside the white chickens." But I like your version better! The other one's too short.

(**HULIE** *just stares at him, devastated.*)

HULIE. Milo, why did you like The Love Song of J. Alfred Prufrock so much?

MILO. Well 'cause it has some pretty zany words. "*Prufrock*"?

HULIE. What about the *meaning*?

MILO. What meaning? Most of it's just nonsense.

SAMANTHA. Hey, he really did forget to say the word "red." *(Shows him the poem.)* Look Milo, see?

MILO. Oh. No wonder you're upset. Can I do it again?

SAMANTHA. Um, Dr. Hulie – I think I just had an amazing idea. Can I talk to you in the hall for sec?

(**SAMANTHA** *and* **HULIE** *exit.* **MILO** *wanders over to the 'Old Woman/Young Woman' optical illusion. He stares at it for a good 10 seconds.*

Then suddenly he sees both images and screams startled. **SAMANTHA** *re-enters.*)

MILO. Don't look at that.

SAMANTHA. What? Oh yeah, isn't that creepy? So, Doctor Hulie's just getting some things for our next exercise.

MILO. Things?

SAMANTHA. Yeah no biggie. Hey, I saw you're doing some sort of show at Fisher Hall?

MILO. Oh yeah. Are you gonna come and try to stump me?

SAMANTHA. Yeah right, I don't think anyone can stump you.

MILO. Yeah, I'm pretty itchy about it already. I might drink some Armagnac beforehand.

SAMANTHA. *(Laughs.)* Yeah right…

MILO. You have a nice pink laugh.

SAMANTHA. Oh. Thank you.

MILO. Yeah in fact you seem *really* pink today.

SAMANTHA. Oh well, I got some good news recently, so.

MILO. What's the good news?

SAMANTHA. Um, so actually I won't be here next semester 'cause I'm doing the Rosenhaas Fellowship.

MILO. Oh hey that's great! But I thought you couldn't apply.

SAMANTHA. Yeah, me too, but then I guess Dr. Hulie miscalculated my G.P.A. or maybe *I* did, I don't know, but anyway, I guess I got panicked over nothing. *(She chuckles.)*

MILO. Wow.

(**DR. HULIE** *comes back in with a large bag.*)

HULIE. I take it she told you what she's doing next semester.

MILO. Yeah, isn't that great!

HULIE. Yes, well before she leaves she had quite an interesting idea actually. Samantha?

SAMANTHA. *(Taking the bag.)* Okay, so basically it's just a fun little exercise for us to do.

MILO. Great, I love fun little exercises.

SAMANTHA. Great. Well the way it works is I'm going to give you a new poem. It's a short one – called The Angel That Presided O'er My Birth.

MILO. Oh I know that one! "That right there's some William Blake!" *(Clears his throat, imitating* **TITO**.*)* "The angel that presided o'er my birth said little creature formed of joy and mirth, go love without the help of any thing on earth."

SAMANTHA. Very good Milo.

MILO. O'er means over.

SAMANTHA. Yes it does. Well what I want you do is just recite it once more. But *very* slowly –

MILO. I can do that.

SAMANTHA. While I play some music.

>   *(***SAMANTHA*** clicks a button. Symphony #40 in G minor Allegro by Mozart starts playing.)*

MILO. *(Nervously.)* What, uh, what are you doing?

SAMANTHA. And while we turn on this red heat lamp.

>   *(***SAMANTHA*** takes out a red heat lamp and turns it on. ***HULIE*** turns off the room light.)*

MILO. I, uh, I'm feeling a little bit nauseous here –

SAMANTHA. And also we're just going to put this nice-smelling Eucalyptus plant right in front of you.

>   *(***SAMANTHA*** takes out a potted Eucalyptus from the shopping bag. She inhales deeply. ***MILO*** starts scratching himself harder.)*

MILO. Dr. Hulie, I think we should stop for the day now.

HULIE. Now don't be nervous Milo. We're just going to try Samantha's experiment for a bit. I want to see what will happen.

MILO. I'll tell you what'll happen – I'm gonna get itchy and sweaty and dizzy is what's happening!

HULIE. Just try it once and then we'll stop, I promise. Just once. Whenever you're ready.

(**MILO** *closes his eyes trying to block it out.*)

MILO. The angel –

SAMANTHA. Open your eyes please Milo.

(**MILO** *opens them and scratches his arm.*)

MILO. The angel hat…hat…the angel that presided odor my, odor my, *o'er* my…

SAMANTHA. Face closer to the plant Milo.

MILO. (*Closing his eyes.*) Odor my, o'er my eyes, my tooth, my ears, my youth, my *youth*!

SAMANTHA. Milo, keep your eyes open!

(**SAMANTHA** *turns up the music.*)

MILO. My youth head, my youth head, my youth said: little fiddle, little fiddle, little fiddle –

(**MILO** *covers his ears.* **SAMANTHA** *walks over and tries to pry his hands off. Finally* **MILO** *screams and knocks over the plant.*)

HULIE. (*To* **SAMANTHA**.) All right Samantha, stop it.

(**SAMANTHA** *stops the music.*)

MILO. Why are you letting her do this to me?

HULIE. Because Milo I think if we clog some of your senses, you'll have room to think about the meaning of the words. You'll exercise different parts of your brain. And if we do this enough –

MILO. We're gonna do this again?!

HULIE. – you'll be able to intuit both the literal and the figurative simultaneously. Just try to get through one recitation this way. It can be a poem or a memory or anything.

MILO. Can't I just memorize stuff? I promise I won't get any words wrong this time!

SAMANTHA. That's really not the point Milo. Let's try it again.

MILO. Seriously don't Samantha!

SAMANTHA. Ready Dr. Hulie?

HULIE. Anything at all, Milo. Just one recitation.

> (**SAMANTHA** *starts the music.* **MILO** *covers his ears.*)

MILO. Our very first session! I came in, Samantha was using your computer, she said you're like really early, I said yeah, where's Dr. Hulie? He's coming, he's in a psych department meeting. Probably discussing the orgasms of four-year-old girls! He discusses things like that? Yes, it arouses him!

> (**HULIE** *shuts off the music.*)

HULIE. *(To* **SAMANTHA.***)* You were using my computer?

SAMANTHA. What? Oh yeah, just for like a sec –

HULIE. Why?

SAMANTHA. Well I was just checking train times really quickly –

MILO. Your email you said.

SAMANTHA. What? No yeah, my email quickly too, my phone was dead.

MILO. You were texting your mom.

SAMANTHA. Well right 'cause it was about to die, and Ida said I could use it so –

MILO. Ida was out to lunch.

SAMANTHA. Obviously before she left, she said I could use the computer quickly, God.

HULIE. *(Grabbing his calendar.)* Our first session was –

MILO. Monday Novermber 18th.

HULIE. Monday November 18th. The same day grades were due to the registrar for the Rosenhaas Fellowship.

SAMANTHA. Oh well I didn't know that. That they were due on the 18th or whatever.

> (**HULIE** *walks over to check his grade book against what's on the computer screen.*)

HULIE. They don't match.

SAMANTHA. What, my grades or something? *(**HULIE** stares at her.)* What, you think I like *snuck* in here and *"tampered"* with your, your whatever on your computer like some sort *"cat burglar"* or something? Dr. Hulie, I don't cheat, okay? And I resent what you're implying! I'm sorry I *happened* to use your computer on the same day that grades *happened* to be due and that you *happened* to miscalculate my midterm, but I am *not* a cheat!

HULIE. How did you know it was the midterm.

SAMANTHA. What? You just said that.

MILO. No he didn't.

HULIE. *(Overlapping.)* No I didn't. I said they don't match. I didn't say what didn't match.

SAMANTHA. Well I just assumed – I mean it counted for the most right? *(**HULIE** stares at her.)* What? *(Starting to cry.)* I didn't do anything!

HULIE. Do you realize how *serious* this is!

SAMANTHA. Please! If you want, I'll do extra credit or something – just let me keep the fellowship!

HULIE. Why would an innocent person want to do extra credit?

SAMANTHA. *(Breaking down.)* Please I'm such a good student! I work so hard! And if I don't do the fellowship, I won't be able to get into a good grad school, I won't be able to start my own practice, I won't have a job, I'll have like *no* money, don't you see? I just wanna be successful and listen to people's problems and write books like you, and do the *This American Life* thing like you, because my mom, she puts so much pressure on me! She's like 'you should have your own TV show like Dr. Phil where you help people with their problems and they'll call in to talk about their marriage, their kids, and yes, their sex-lives, but also their bosses and their co-workers, their *pets*, whatever," and I'm like 'I don't even want that! I'm not *about* the grade! I just care about the work' but she's like *intent* on me having a future where, like, the cops call me when they're looking for a criminal, 'cause I'll know about personalities, and tell them where the murderers are hiding just from looking at their handwriting on ransom notes and it's a lot of pressure because all I want to do is just help people and make this horrible disgusting putrid world where everyone hates each other and dies sad and alone just a little bit better and is that so *wrong*?!

(SAMANTHA cries. HULIE just stares at her.)

HULIE. I'm reporting you to the Dean's office immediately.

SAMANTHA. No please! My mom – my mom's on the board of the New York Psychoanalytic Institute. They have tons of grant money. They can help you with so many projects!

HULIE. Are you attempting to bribe me?

SAMANTHA. What? No! I'm just saying they can help you out. Unrelated.

HULIE. You spoiled little brat! You've been given everything in life. *Everything!* And it's not enough for you. You need to lie, cheat, and steal your way to the top. You are *everything* that's wrong with the youth today. With the entire…the, the youth of America!

SAMANTHA. What? *America?* There are kids in gangs who kill each other and rape women every day!

HULIE. They weren't given the advantages you were! *(He points to MILO.) He* wasn't given the advantages you were! And yet he comes in here every week and works his butt off!

SAMANTHA. He *doesn't* work his butt off! He was born a freak of nature! *I* work my butt off!

HULIE. Tell your mother on the board of the New York Psychoanalytic Institute that she should expect a call from the Dean of Deans College. I'd talk to her myself but I'm afraid of all the disappointing things I'd say about her daughter.

(HULIE exits. MILO sits there awkwardly.)

MILO. That's funny: "The Dean of Deans."

(**SAMANTHA** *looks up at* **MILO**, *seething.*)

SAMANTHA. Do you know what you just did?

MILO. I was gonna say, did I say something I shouldn't have?

SAMANTHA. You just *ruined my entire life,* you fucking…freak!

MILO. Well it looks like you're seeing a lot of yellowish-blue right now, so maybe you shoul –

SAMANTHA. No I'm not seeing any "*yellowish-blue!*" I'm feeling *emotions,* emotions called anger and pain and misery! Do you know what anger and pain and misery are, you idiot?!

MILO. *(Quietly.)* Yes.

SAMANTHA. I don't think you do. I don't think you realize there's a whole world around you that's not on your little color wheel! Well fine. 'Cause if someone does to you what you just did to me, you're gonna taste it, and touch it, and feel it, and smell it, and you won't be able to figure out *what* color you're feeling, and guess what: you're gonna be fucked.

MILO. Actually on Thanksgiving Gina kissed me on the cheek, so I think I'm gonna be fine. Now is Dr. Hulie gonna come back or should I go get something to eat?

SAMANTHA. *(Chuckles.)* Y'know something? I really hope you're right. 'Cause if someone ever does hurt you, you'll never ever *ever* forget it.

(*She walks out of the office. Lights out.*)

End of Act 1

ACT 2

Scene 1

*(An empty stage with a curtain drawn. **TITO** walks out holding a microphone.)*

TITO. Thanks for coming out to the show y'all. And now please welcome… Milo Mazowski, i.e., – The Mehnemonist Of Dutchess County!

*(**MILO** comes out.)*

MILO. Oh, I checked with Dr. Hulie, it's *Mnemonist.*

*(**TITO** pulls out a deck of cards.)*

TITO. All right yo, you all ready for this?

(He starts humming a song in the style of "Get Ready For This" as he goes into the crowd.)*

All right what's your name.

(An audience member says their name.)

All right *(Insert name.)*, you know how to shuffle a deck of cards?

(The person says yes.)

Well then shuffle away, yo.

(The person shuffles them.)

---

*A license to produce *The Mnemonist of Dutchess County* does not include a performance license for "Get Ready for This." The publisher and author suggest that the licensee contact ASCAP or BMI to ascertain the rights holder to acquire permission for performance of this song. If permission is unattainable, the licensee should create an original composition in a similar style. For further information, please see music use note on page 3

Damn, you got good technique but you're slow. Sorry, no rush. Take your time.

> *(She gives* **TITO** *back the cards.)*

Let's give it up for *(Name)*! Hold this, miss.

> *(***TITO*** *hands her the mic and searches his jacket for a flower. He hands her the flower and takes back the mic. He hands the cards to* **MILO***.)*

All right y'all, he's got thirty seconds to memorize these, so time him. In the meantime I'm gonna freestyle.

> *(***TITO*** *freestyles with the person's name for a few seconds. Followed by polite applause.)*

Yeah that's right. He ain't the only talented guy up here. Okay, give me the cards Milo.

> *(***TITO*** *takes the cards.)*

All right now he's gonna say 'em in order. Ready Milo? Go!

> *(***MILO*** *freezes.)*

Milo, c'mon, go!

MILO. Uh, jack of hearts, 6 of clubs, 5 of clubs, king of clubs, 10 of diamonds, jack of diamonds, queen of spades, 3 of diamonds, 10 of spades, 7 of diamonds, 10 of clubs, 7 of spades, 5 of spades, King of hearts –

TITO. That's me, yo, I'm the King of Hearts.

MILO. Three of spades, 8 of diamonds, 9 of diamonds, 4 of diamonds, jack of spades, 8 of hearts, ace of clubs, ace of hearts, 4 of hearts, 6 of spades, 8 of spades, 9 of hearts, 5 of diamonds, 6 of diamonds, queen of diamonds, jack of clubs, 8 of clubs, 2 of spades, 4 of clubs, 2 of diamonds, Queen of hearts –

TITO. That's you miss, you're the Queen of Hearts.

MILO. Nine of spades, 7 of clubs, queen of clubs, 2 of hearts, 3 of clubs, 2 of clubs, 6 of hearts, ace of diamonds, 5 of hearts, 10 of hearts, 4 of spades, 9 of clubs, 3 of hearts, King of spades, 7 of hearts, ace of spades, King of...

(**MILO** *pauses for effect as if he's forgotten.*) …just kidding, Diamonds.

TITO. Yeah, son! Yo let's hear it for the Meh-nemonist –

MILO. It's actually *Mnemonist.*

TITO. You sure?

MILO. Yes.

TITO. All right, The *Mnemonist* of Dutchess County!

(*Lights out.*)

Scene 2

(The Blind Eagle. Later that night. **MILO** *and* **TITO** *sit in the back room, playing chess. They're both drunk. Sounds of a crowded bar emanate from the front room.)*

MILO. *(Drunkenly.)* I don't understand – how come this piece can only move diagonally? I want to move forward.

TITO. That's just the rules. Here use this piece.

*(***MILO*** does. ***TITO*** moves in response.)*

Checkmate.

MILO. What? I lost?

TITO. Yeah, son – you gotta protect your King. I can't believe you never played chess before.

MILO. It's too black and white. This game needs more color.

TITO. Here drink this, it'll give it more color.

*(***TITO*** hands ***MILO*** a shot.)*

To a sold-out show! Tito Davis and Milo Mazowski – partners in crime!

MILO. Two birds and a stone!

(They drink. **GINA** *comes in with a fancy bottle of booze. She's also drunk.)*

GINA. There he is! I brought some good stuff for the star of the night!

TITO. Hey, it's the *stars* of the night. That shit is plural.

GINA. *(To* **MILO**.*)* Ooh somebody's jealous.

TITO. Yo, I *made* my money – I ain't jealous.

*(***GINA*** sits on ***MILO***'s lap.)*

GINA. How 'bout now?

TITO. Do what you want.

GINA. "Oh, do what you want."

MILO. You gonna pour that stuff or keep talking?

GINA. Look at you, all diva-ish now!

MILO. I'm the Diva of Dutchess County! Diva wants his booze!

TITO. Yo, who's watching the door?

GINA. Uhhhhhh…

TITO. Shit, now *I'm* the responsible one?

(**TITO** *gets up and exits to the front.*)

MILO. Hey you wanna play chess? Tito just taught me.

GINA. No, you're gonna kill me.

MILO. I'm terrible, I just learned! Did you know that this piece can only move diagonally? And this one? It can only move in an L shape! Whaaat?

(**GINA** *laughs.*)

(*Setting up his chess pieces.*) You have an amazing laugh. You weren't at my show.

GINA. I know, I had to open the bar. I was so bummed!

MILO. Me too. I was hoping you'd look at me in awe.

GINA. What you mean like this?

(*She pretends to look at him in awe. He giggles. They start playing chess.*)

MILO. You know what I need? A mentor at chess. Will you be my mentor?

GINA. I don't come cheap.

MILO. I'll pay anything.

GINA. I'm very busy.

MILO. Just one game a day.

GINA. I don't know if I can fit it in.

MILO. That's what she said. Ohhhh!

(**GINA** *looks at him, actually in awe.*)

GINA. (*Playfully accusatory.*) You're changing.

MILO. (*Holding his glass up.*) To change!

GINA. To a change of scenery.

MILO. To you staying.

GINA. To me leaving.

MILO. If you go, who's gonna be my mentor?

(**JOEY** *enters, holding a flyer.*)

Joey Broey!

JOEY. What the fuck is this?

MILO. That's a flyer to my show! Tito's got one planned in Vermont next week. And then our tour continues to Vassar and a couple more after that – you gonna come?

JOEY. No, I'm not gonna fucking come.

(*They both stop and look at him.*)

GINA. Geez, somebody's in a bad mood.

JOEY. I was in a fine mood until I saw this shit. The fuck are you doing?

MILO. What do you mean? I'm performing for people.

JOEY. So what, you wanna be a sideshow freak now? I took you to that shrink guy so he could help you with this shit. Not so you could get worse!

MILO. How am I getting worse?

JOEY. How are you – ? Jesus Milo, 'cause you're fucking… indulging your problem.

MILO. "Indulging my problem"?

JOEY. Yes! You're making your mind more screwy instead of fixing it!

MILO. Well I don't know why I'd need to "fix it" 'cause it wasn't broken.

JOEY. Oh, so what? You thought you got fired for no reason at all? And nobody will hire you again why? Y'know, I thought you could change but you can't. Thought it'd be nice if I didn't have to take care of you all the time.

GINA. Joey, that's a rotten thing to say.

JOEY. What, it's true.

MILO. Whaaat? You don't *"take care"* of me. I can "take care" of myself. Look see? *(He holds up the cash.)* I made a lot of money tonight!

JOEY. Yeah, 'cause you sold yourself out. You let Tito take advantage of you. And y'know something – if *anyone's* gonna be making money off you, it should be me.

MILO. Oh so you need money.

JOEY. *No!* I'm just saying, I'm the one who broke my back dealing with you for years.

MILO. Oh you were "dealing" with me? And here I thought we were friends.

JOEY. You know what I mean! Or maybe you don't, I don't know. Maybe you don't realize that a shrink's supposed to make you normal, not turn you into more of a mutant.

GINA. Stop it, Joey. You're being an asshole.

JOEY. I'm just being honest. And you're one to talk. Leading him on like you do.

GINA. *Excuse me?*

JOEY. You heard me. And don't pretend you don't know what I'm talking about. Giving him false hope with your, your fucking 'baby talk.'

GINA. Oh you're really reaching here.

MILO. Yeah you're…*reaching.*

JOEY. Oh don't think we all haven't seen how you look at her Milo. And I'm sorry but just to be honest? Neither her nor any other sane girl would ever touch you with a ten-foot pole.

GINA. *Joe!* Go home, you're drunk.

JOEY. I'm not drunk. I've barely had some drinks or two.

MILO. No, you know what you are? *(MILO stands up.)* You're blue with envy.

JOEY. *(Sighs.)* Jesus Christ Milo. You mean green with envy and no I'm not.

MILO. Yes you are. Look at you. Your whole face is turning blue with envy.

JOEY. Milo, you fucking idiot, the phrase is "green with envy."

GINA. Guys.

(MILO *goes right up to* JOEY.)

MILO. You're totally jealous and you can't admit it.

JOEY. Never in a million years would I be jealous of you.

MILO. But you are. You're totally blue.

JOEY. It's green.

MILO. Look at you. You're bitter and you're jealous and you resent me and you're blue.

JOEY. IT'S GREEN!

(JOEY *punches* MILO. MILO *stumbles backwards.* JOEY *grabs his hand in pain.*)

Fuck!

GINA. Oh my God, are you crazy?

JOEY. Fuck!

(JOEY *storms out.*)

GINA. Joey get back here! (GINA *goes to* MILO.) Are you okay?

MILO. I just need to sit down.

(MILO *dizzily stumbles into a chair.*)

GINA. Let me see. Stay right there, I'll get an ice pack.

(GINA *runs out.* MILO *closes his eyes.*)

MILO. (*Counting to himself.*) 104, 105, 106, 107…104, 105, 106, 107…

(SAMANTHA *stumbles in from the front. She's exceptionally drunk.*)

(*Opening his eyes.*) Oh no…

SAMANTHA. Well lookie who it is. Mr. Memory himself. I heard you performed quite the feats tonight. Some *fallacial* feats!

MILO. That's not a word.

SAMANTHA. It's a word! It means *you.* Listen, can I sit down? *(She sits on the floor next to him.)* I've had a night of reflection tonight. You have strong calves.

MILO. Thanks. Thank you.

SAMANTHA. Oh my God, you do. But listen. Tonight is now winter break. And thanks to you I don't know if I'm coming back next semester 'cause I need to go to a disciplinary trial. But what I'm saying is, it's *not* thanks to you, it's thanks on *me.* 'Cause I overreacted.

MILO. Okay.

SAMANTHA. No, *not* okay! I really shouldn't have screamed in your face. 'Cause it's not like any of that was *your* fault. It's not your fault that I didn't make the grade. It's not your fault that I cheated. And it's not your fault that if I'm going down, I'm going down with a bang tonight and I bought myself some Klonopins, booya! Anyway really sorry.

MILO. Wait, what?

SAMANTHA. Yeah, you want some Klonopins? Too late, I took 'em all! I'm gonna take a nappy nap now. *(She lies down.)* I think I need to puke again, but I'll do it when I get up, 'mkay?

MILO. Uhh…somebody?

*(**TITO** comes in and sees **SAMANTHA**.)*

TITO. Jesus Christ, there she is. Dude this is bad. She puked all over the dance floor.

SAMANTHA. *You* puked all over the pants-floor. Hey aren't you the guy who sold me those Klonopins?

TITO. Shit. Uh sweetie? How many did you take?

SAMANTHA. I ate them all, is that all right? I don't care. I need a doctor of medicine maybe.

TITO. Oh shit, this is bad. *(**TITO** gets down next to her.)* Sweetie, I'm gonna lift you up okay?

*(**TITO** lifts her up.)*

SAMANTHA. Ooh fun. I'm spinny. I'm gonna go sleep now.

TITO. Don't fall asleep! *(Shouting.)* Somebody call an ambulance!

> *(TITO carries her out. MILO counts to himself again. GINA comes in with an ice pack.)*

GINA. Don't worry about Joey. He drank too much tonight. I drank too much tonight. Here, hold this there. Oh Milo, your lip's bleeding.

> *(She grabs a napkin and wipes MILO's lip.)*

MILO. It's okay. I have a system in place to take my mind off the pain. I count from 104 to 107 over and over again.

GINA. *(Chuckles.)* What?

MILO. Yeah. Those numbers calm me down. 107 reminds me of you actually.

GINA. *(Chuckles.)* Really? Why?

MILO. 'Cause it's amazing. See, 100 is an orange sunset with the two big zeroes there. And seven is a beautiful woman, wearing a dark purple dress. That's my favorite color. Dark Purple. And together they show this dark purple woman lying quietly on the beach at sunset, as the orange-crimson sky gets darker and darker and darker. It's my favorite number. 107.

> *(She looks at him, getting sucked in.)*

GINA. You see those images for every number?

MILO. Every number. Every word.

GINA. What do you see for 87?

MILO. Eighty-seven's a fat woman holding a cat.

> *(GINA dabs his lip with the napkin.)*

GINA. Twenty-two.

MILO. A pair of ducks in the water.

> *(GINA moves closer. She takes the napkin off and feels his lip with her finger.)*

GINA. One thousand six hundred and seven.

MILO. A baby in a sports jacket. *(They're inches away.)* With a mustache and a cane.

GINA. That's crazy.

MILO. I know.

GINA. You're crazy.

MILO. I can't help it.

  (They kiss. Lights out.)

Scene 3

*(An empty stage with the curtain drawn. **TITO**
walks out, but this time with a more expensive
head mic on. There's a blackboard center stage.)*

TITO. Once again put your hands together for the one, the
only… Milo Mazowski… The Mnemonist of Dutchess
County!

> *(Thunderous applause. **MILO** comes out,
> pretending to be upset.)*

Whoa, Milo buddy what's wrong.

MILO. I can't remember anything! I forgot where I live,
where I'm from… I can't even remember my own
name!

TITO. Damn – how long you been having this problem?

MILO. What problem?

> *(Drum hit. **MILO** and **TITO** mug for the audience.
> **TITO** goes over to the board.)*

TITO. All right this is what we're gonna do. Milo here's
gonna put on a blindfold. **(MILO** *does.)* He can't see
through that shit. Now I want y'all to just shout the
day of the month you were born on. Like if you were
born on December 25th, you say 25. Got it? All right,
go ahead let's hear 'em.

> *(People shout out some numbers. **TITO** repeats
> them as they're said and writes them on the board.)*

Okay, yo that's enough. The guy can remember a lot
but he can't remember that much.

MILO. I don't care. Keep going.

TITO. Would you cut it out? C'mon man.

MILO. No, give me a few more. I have an *unlimited* memory!

TITO. All right, yo, a few more.

> *(People shout out more. They're added.)*

Okay cool, that's enough. Now I need a volunteer. You. Yes you hotstuff, c'mon up.

(**TITO** *pulls someone on stage.*)

You nervous? *(They nod.)* Good. Well all you gotta do is just stand there and look pretty. Milo? Pull up the blindfold and peep at this hottie. (**MILO** *does so.*) Now put it back on. (**MILO** *does so.* **TITO** *turns to the person.*) All right, just hang out back there yo. *(He points to a spot downstage where the audience can see them.)*

(**TITO** *pulls out a large piece of white paper.*)

This here's a blank piece of paper. And this here's a pencil. I don't know, he's a weird guy – he likes to draw when he recalls shit. Milo here.

(**TITO** *hands* **MILO** *the paper and pencil.*)

Yo, pull up the blindfold a little. A *little.* (**MILO** *does so.*) Now what were those numbers?

(**MILO** *recites the numbers as he draws, focusing only on the paper. He finishes.*)

Pretty good – yo, what's that you drew?

(**MILO** *holds up a perfect portrait of the person he saw for a second.* **TITO** *holds it up next to the person so the audience can see the resemblance. They gasp?*)

Isn't this guy annoying? Yo, tell your friends!

(Lights out.)

Scene 4

*(The Blind Eagle. **GINA** sits in the mostly cleaned out bar. **JOEY** reads a citation.)*

JOEY. *(Reading.)* "The New York State Liquor Authority hereby suspends the license of Giamani LTD. doing business as "The Blind Eagle Pub" at 66 Broadway in the Village of Tivoli. The SLA charged the bar with eighteen violations, including underage sales, prescription drugs being distributed to minors on premises, unlicensed bouncers..." *(He looks up at **GINA**, then keeps going.)* "...and excessive noise. The bar was previously fined by the SLA for $4,000, and $8,000 for similar infractions, the balance of which has not yet been paid. Effective immediately, there is a lien on the property and no alcohol may be served or consumed on the premises." *(He stops.)* I know a cop in the traffic department. *(He shrugs.)*

*(**TITO** walks in, guiltily. **JOEY** looks at him.)*

Well you really fucking fucked up.

*(**JOEY** hits him with his shoulder as he exits.)*

TITO. Baby, I'm sorry. *(No response.)* It wasn't my fault though. *(No response.)* Baby c'mon.

GINA. Don't call me baby. Okay?

*(She starts gathering bottles. **TITO** sighs.)*

TITO. All right look – it *was* my fault. Okay? You're right. I fucked up. It's my job to check ID's...and whatever, I guess that night I let the ball hit the ground. Didn't keep my eyes on the prize sort of deal. But honestly, I swear on my mother, I had no idea you were selling this place. *(Scoffs.)* And thanks for telling me by the way. See I got hurt in this deal too.

GINA. Your mother called by the way.

*(**TITO** freezes.)*

TITO. Shit.

GINA. Yeah shit's right. "Oh Ms. Davis, so nice to finally meet you albeit over the phone. How's your back doing?" "My back? It's fine, why?" "Didn't you have a couple of surgeries?" "A *couple*?! Thank God, I never had *any*!"

TITO. She has chronic back pain I swear! Look I needed the job so I exaggerated. I wanted to go legit!

GINA. Go "legit"?! Jesus, you're nothing but a degenerate, drug-dealing liar. *(Reaching for her necklace.)* Here, you can take this back.

*(**GINA** takes off her Topaz necklace.)*

TITO. C'mon Gina don't do that – I got that for you.

GINA. Yeah well it's ugly and I don't want to pretend it's not anymore. Okay?

TITO. Oh whatever. *(Snorts.)* Didn't pay nothing for it anyway.

GINA. Excuse me?

TITO. Nothing.

GINA. What, you stole it? Or let me guess: you traded it for drugs.

TITO. What? No! Actually I found it all right? 'Cause –

GINA. Ah ah ah, I don't want to hear your voice anymore.

*(**GINA** gathers more bottles. **TITO** walks right in front of her.)*

TITO. *(Exaggerated.)* How's this: *I'm. Sorry.* Okay you little princess?

(She slaps him. He just stands there.)

You're a real piece of work, y'know that?

*(**GINA** slams the garbage bag down.)*

GINA. Oh *I'm* a piece of work?! You almost got a girl *killed!* By selling pills to her in MY bar! And I didn't even fucking know about it until the cops told me – right before taking my liquor license away because on top of everything else she was *underage!* So now I have nothing! Absolutely nothing! I can't sell the bar, I can't run the bar! I can only sit here and listen to you tell me it's not your fault, which it fucking is!

TITO. Yo maybe they'll still buy it. I mean they're rich-ass pricks right?

> *(She picks up the bag and exits out the back. **TITO** steals a bottle with some booze left in it. He gets up and leaves as **MILO** enters.)*

MILO. Hey where you going? It's our first night back, I thought we were drinking!

> *(**TITO** doesn't come back. **MILO** sits down. **GINA** re-enters. She sees **MILO** and stops.)*

Taking the trash out?

GINA. Um, yeah.

> *(They both nod. Silence.)*

GINA.	**MILO.**
So how was – sorry you go first.	I kept trying to –

MILO. Oh, no I was just gonna say I kept trying to call you while I was away but I guess –

GINA. Oh yeah, I got really busy with, um, the police, so…

MILO. Yeah I mean I was feeling a little itchy about it 'cause I kept calling, but, y'know it's fine. Oh! You should've seen it though – there was so much snow around Bennington in Vermont that my feet were soaking wet when I performed and it kept causing me to invert numbers and colors and say 'R' words like 'W' words –

GINA. Yeah, no I got your texts where you said all that.

MILO. Oh right yeah, I just didn't know if you saw to it or not. Also someone asked me to recite Hamlet and the heater was on and it was really loud and the room smelled wet so I started "it was the best of times, it was the worst of times –

GINA. Right, yeah, I got that one too. Sorry for not texting you back, things were just crazy –

MILO. Oh, yeah it's totally fine. I should tell you the rest though.

GINA. Yeah actually I'm sort of tired.

MILO. Oh sure, okay.

>(**MILO** *picks up a bottle of Armagnac.*)

Eh? Eh?

GINA. Oh um, no thanks.

MILO. But we gotta celebrate.

GINA. *(Gently.)* Yeah, not tonight. Congrats on your little tour though.

MILO. What? No, I mean we gotta celebrate you. 'Cause I heard the good news. You're staying! *(Beat.)* Y'know 'cause of…

GINA. Yeah, no I know. It's not really good news though is it?

MILO. Sure it is! It means we finally get to be together.

GINA. Um. Listen. Milo, let's um…why don't we sit for a second.

>(*She sits. He goes for a kiss. She moves away.*)

So listen, that night was – I mean I had a really fun time –

MILO. Yeah, me too. Wait, you mean that night before I left when we had sex?

GINA. Yeah, yes –

MILO. Yeah, me too.

>(*He goes to kiss her again, she pulls away again.*
>*They both chuckle awkwardly.*)

(Chuckling.) You keep doing that.

GINA. *(Chuckling.)* Yeah. So listen Milo – I've known you for so long… And obviously I love you and everything –

MILO. I love you too.

GINA. No I – *(she clears her throat.)* What I mean is, um… I love being friends with you.

MILO. Yeah right – me too.

GINA. Well and so let's not ruin anything, 'cause I think you're so great and I just really want to keep our friendship, y'know? Because you're such a great guy and y'know it was just a crazy, drunken night and sort of a mistake so I don't want to ruin things and make them uncomfortable, okay? Is that okay?

MILO. *(Starting to get it.)* Wait. What are you...you're saying –

GINA. No, I'm just saying we were *so* drunk, and let's just, y'know, laugh about it and move on.

MILO. Laugh about it?

GINA. No, I just mean y'know, obviously we wouldn't work together in *that* way, that's all.

MILO. In what way. The romantic way?

GINA. Ye – yeah. The romantic way. Which is totally fine –

MILO. Why not.

GINA. Well y'know – we just *wouldn't*. We're from different places and –

MILO. No we're not, we're from the same place. We're both from here.

GINA. Milo, I'm sorry, okay? It's just the way I feel.

MILO. Can you just tell me *WHY* though?!

GINA. Okay, well, I mean, what – you wanna know why *exactly*?

MILO. Yes! That's what I want to know! I want to know *why EXACTLY!*

GINA. Okay, well lots of reasons! I mean first off, that night, I just, I thought I was leaving. And so I acted recklessly okay? And I can't do that anymore because I gotta figure a lot of shit out – I mean a girl almost died in here and her mom is up my ass and so are the cops –

MILO. Oh wait, you mean Samantha? *(Chuckles.)* Oh wow, you had me so worried. No it's okay, she was just trying to hurt me.

GINA. What?

MILO. Yeah 'cause she made me smell a plant and I hurt her feelings, so then I guess she took those pills to make *you* mad so you would try to hurt *my* feelings, but just don't pay any attention to her and we can be together.

GINA. Okay, but it doesn't have to do with her.

MILO. No yeah it does.

GINA. It really doesn't.

MILO. It does. It's her fault.

GINA. It isn't.

MILO. Whose is it then, Tito?

GINA. It's *YOU* Milo! Okay? *You!* We're not compatible for lots of reasons, okay? Jesus! I mean first of all you're just really literal 'cause of the way your mind works, which is not your fault, but I can't just sit there and listen to you recount how your feet were wet for like half an hour, it's like am I even here? I'm sorry but the things you find interesting, I don't find interesting, and I'm glad you like movies and books, I do too, but I don't want to hear them recited in their entirety, I just *can't*, I can't do it – and it's great that you're so passionate about remembering every detail of life, and seeing the patterns in things, but you're actually missing a lot because you're so focused on the details, you don't see the important stuff, and I just can't be with someone who is *that* focused on such minute meaningless bullshit and who recites it to me for hours on end 'cause quite frankly, I'm getting older now and it's a *waste of time,* and I would've felt this way regardless of what happened to that girl Samantha, I just wouldn't have *said* it to you 'cause I'd be *gone* but now I'm here and you made me say it, and so I'm sorry, but I don't like you in that way, okay?

MILO. *(Rubs his cheek.)* Ow.

GINA. God, don't hate me. I shouldn't have said that. Urrhh, why am I like this? See, it's me.

MILO. You really…you really just broke a lot of glass on my face.

GINA. What? No, I didn't mean to…

(**MILO** *rubs his face.*)

MILO. Why did you…you just – what did I do to make you break so much glass on my face?

GINA. Oh God, nothing Milo! You didn't *do* anything! I didn't mean to –

MILO. *(Tearing up.)* You didn't mean it right?

GINA. I…well yeah I meant what I said but I didn't mean –

MILO. *(Tearing up.)* Well stop it! Stop telling me why I'm so bad to be around and take this glass out of my face!

GINA. I didn't mean to hurt you. I didn't mean to…break glass on your face.

MILO. *(Starting to cry.)* Well you did so stop it!

(**GINA** *goes to hug him.*)

GINA. Milo I still –

MILO. Don't touch me! Don't come near me! *(He tries to compose himself.)* How could you say those words to me? I would never say those words to you!

GINA. I know. You're great. And I'm so sorry.

(*She takes his hand and rubs it. He lets her.*)

MILO. C'mon just…

(**MILO** *tries to kiss her. She turns away.*)

GINA. No Milo. I'm sorry. *(Beat.)* But we can't do that anymore.

(**MILO** *nods, trying not to cry. He walks out holding his face. Lights out.*)

Scene 5

(An empty stage. **TITO** *comes out wearing his head mike and a "Mnemonist of Dutchess County" T-shirt.)*

TITO. What up everyone! Y'all have a good New Year's?

(People give various responses.)

Yeah I guess it was like a while ago. Anyway glad y'all could get into the show. And sorry to y'all that couldn't. *(Beat.)* Although obviously those folks ain't here, so I don't know why I'm talking to them. Anyway please welcome back to the stage the one, the only, Milo Mazowski... The Mnemonist of Dutchess County!

(Thunderous applause. **MILO** *comes out. He looks out of it.* **TITO** *wheels out a row of books on a wheelie thing.)*

All right y'all, I got some books here. The Encyclopedia Britannica series Volumes 1 through 19. Each with over *a thousand* pages. Now I'm gonna close my eyes and move my finger and you tell me when to stop.

(He moves his finger, someone yells stop.)

Okay, volume 16 it is. Now somebody yell out a page number.

(Somebody yells out a page number, let's say 702.)

Let's see here...700...and 2...found it. *(Beat.)* Milo: what does it say on page 702.

*(***MILO****'s breathes rapidly.)*

MILO. Jack of hearts, six of clubs, ten of diamonds, seven of spades –

TITO. What? Uh... *(Laughs nervously.)* he's just messing. *(Quietly.)* Milo, page 702. You got this.

*(***MILO*** *stares straight ahead like a deer in headlights.)*

MILO. It, uh…it was the best of times, it was the worst times, the age of wisdom…foolishness?

TITO. That uh, that's Dickens *(To the audience.)* you shoulda seen it, yo, he recited the whole book one show! *(Quietly to* **MILO.***)* C'mon buddy, you know this. 702. Volume 14.

> **(MILO** *looks around panicked.)*

(Quietly.) You got this Milo. C'mon! 702…

> **(MILO** *closes his eyes trying to escape. He breathes heavily. Then he opens his eyes.)*

MILO. Shih Tzu – a breed of small companion dog of very ancient dog type, with long silky fur.

> **(TITO** *sighs relieved. He holds up the book to show the audience. They clap politely.)*

Originated in China, possibly by way of Tibet. The name is both singular and plural.

TITO. Ain't that something folks? All right someone give me another page number –

MILO. One of the smallest breeds of dog, The Shih Tzu was almost completely wiped out during the Chinese Revolution –

TITO. All right cool. Shih Tzu. Moving on.

MILO. Thus they are often called "Small Survivors," "Friendly lap dogs."

TITO. *(Chuckling.)* Okay, you finished there buddy?

MILO. While there is no such thing as a "toy sized" Shih Tzu, there is an *Imperial* Shih Tzu which is a term used by breeders to sell Shih Tzu that are below healthy standard size. Often 50% below. They are too small. Way too small. Unhealthily small. Like little pieces of minutiae that burrow into your home and never leave. That plague you every day and night, in your dreams, when you're sleeping, causing you to forget the *(Air quotes.)* "important stuff" of life. So whatever you do, do *not* invite the little teeny tiny minutiae shit into your house, ladies and gentlemen. Or you will never. Ever.

Ever. Get rid of it. *(He turns to* **TITO**.*)* And now I'm finished. Next page ladies and gentlemen.

TITO. The, uh…the Mnemonist of Dutchess County.

(Lights out.)

Scene 6

(HULIE's office. MILO sits in the dark. The toilet flushes. HULIE exits the bathroom.)

MILO. What's this.

HULIE. *(Startled.)* Jesus, Milo! You scared the living daylights out of me. I thought we weren't meeting today.

MILO. What's this.

(MILO holds up a piece of paper.)

HULIE. That? That, uh, looks like the speech I gave at the Symposium in –

MILO. The New York Psycho-Analytic Symposium. See, it says it right here on the top. And did your speech go well?

HULIE. Yes – funny enough I got a standing ovation. The moderator actually had to tell people to –

MILO. *(Reading.)* "M as I like to call him has quite the gift for memory…"

HULIE. Yes well, perhaps we should uh discuss –

MILO. "However, his unstable grasp of reality, coupled with the quixotic nature" – mmm 'quixotic.'

HULIE. It uh…it means sort of 'impractical.'

MILO. It means 'irrational' or 'foolish.' "…Coupled with the *foolish* nature of his fantasies had a profound effect on his personality or lack thereof."

HULIE. Now Milo, you have to understand –

MILO. "It was precisely this misguided alacrity" – again, why are you using words like *alacrity?*

HULIE. Well it means –

MILO. I KNOW what it means. "It was precisely this misguided *eagerness*" – see, it's so much better – "This misguided eagerness that led people to take him for a dull, awkward, somewhat absentminded fellow. No one had the heart to tell him that the way he saw the world did not coincide with the way the world actually was."

Why are you speaking in the past tense? Isn't the way I see the world *still* in fact not the way the world really *IS*?

HULIE. I understand why you're upset.

MILO. Oh do you? Do you understand why? Do you understand why someone like me who had promises made to him – promises that were *not* kept – would be upset?

HULIE. Well I don't think that's true about the promises –

MILO. Oh really? And I quote: "What I'm prepared to do, Milo, is help you figure out why those people are laughing and how to become more socially comfortable, so that you can make new friends and have better relationships with the ones you *do* have."

HULIE. All right point taken, but what I said in my speech doesn't mean I broke that promise.

MILO. Mmm, yes it does, because you wanted to insult me and take advantage of me this whole time, and now all my friends hate me.

HULIE. That's not true Milo, and I very much doubt your friends hate you.

MILO. Well one of them punched me in the face and another said she doesn't want to see me anymore because I'm too focused on "minute meaningless bullshit," so you're wrong.

HULIE. Milo, I'm – I'm sorry. What happened? Would you like to talk about it?

MILO. Why, so you can make fun of me and then get a standing ovation?

HULIE. I didn't mean for you to see that speech and perhaps, yes, I could have been a little gentler but then –

MILO. But then it wouldn't have sold as many books right? No, I'm catching on – you've definitely made me more aware of the "*nuances*" of social situations.

HULIE. You have to believe me when I say I didn't mean to hurt you.

MILO. Yeah I've been hearing a lot of that lately. Oh, I almost forgot, here's a fun tidbit: "One of the purported reasons why M first came to me was because of the recent death of his mother" –

HULIE. All right that's enough –

MILO. Why is it enough?! Did you NOT read this part out loud?! *(HULIE's silent.)* "One of the purported reasons why M first came to me was because of the recent death of his mother – although to call him 'depressed' would be a funny and misleading nomer" – again, "*nomer*"? – "As the only mention of her and the pancreatic cancer she died from was stated matter-of-factly in passing and devoid of any discernible human emotion."

HULIE. Let me explain –

MILO. No let ME explain! First off, I didn't realize your goal was to make me as yellow and nauseous as possible – if I'd realized that I would've talked your ear off about my mom and given you more material for your stupid pointless book. Second of all, my mom lives out in Florida – excuse me, *lived* out in Florida – and when she was in the final stages of her cancer she told me not to come and visit her and that she would write me letters instead so I wouldn't have to see her or hear her while she rotted away!

HULIE. I'm sorry I didn't know that. But all I was trying to say is that that's a tad *unusual.*

MILO. Yeah for you because you don't remember things like I do! I hear the voice of someone dying and I will see it, smell it, touch it, taste it, and I will NEVER EVER forget it. Do you understand that?! So please excuse my mom for not wanting me to go and visit her so I could take detailed mental notes about the way she looked and smelt as she rotted that I could give to you for your book!

(**MILO** *sniffles and looks away.* **HULIE** *doesn't know what to say.*)

HULIE. Milo I've made it my life's work to help people like you, and I'm so sorry that thus far I haven't. But I still want to try to help if you'll let me.

MILO. You think you can help me?

HULIE. I *can* help you.

(**MILO** *grabs* **HULIE** *by his collar.*)

MILO. Well then make me forget!

HULIE. Milo, let go please –

MILO. MAKE ME FORGET!

HULIE. Milo, you're hurting me.

MILO. I hurt every day, every *second.* Every single second I feel every single one of my memories like it's happening *right now,* so make me forget!

HULIE. I can't! You're just going to have to live with your memories like everyone else, all right?!

(**MILO** *lets go. He slumps down his chair.*)

MILO. (*He sniffles.*) I, uh, I tried that writing technique where I write things down and throw them away, but it doesn't work anymore. I tried writing an entire conversation I had with Gina down and burning the paper. But I just saw the words in the embers. I can remember things with music playing now. With red lights and smelly plants. Nothing even distracts me anymore. The only thing I can't do is forget.

(**HULIE** *sits next to* **MILO.**)

HULIE. Listen Milo: I don't like kids. I never have and I never will. But my wife adores them. She's always wanted them. So we fought about having them, small debates at first, then huge heated fights. She threw a plate at my head. I slept on the couch. I slept in a hotel. I even slept in Newburgh one night. I hated, I mean *hated* the idea of raising kids so much that in fact I slept in Newburgh on multiple occasions. But finally

I thought, well I *hate* kids but not more than I love my wife. So we tried for months. Finally she got pregnant. She was overjoyed in a way I've never seen her before. We bought a new house in Rhinebeck that had a bigger room for the baby. We spent days and weeks painting the house one color, then she wasn't happy so we painted it *another* color. Then eight months in she had a miscarriage. Not only that but the doctors had to perform emergency surgery to try and save the baby. And during the surgery her Fallopian tubes were damaged. And we found out she was now unable to ever have children. And she was devastated. More devastated then I've ever seen anybody in my life. She was a walking zombie. And you know what *I* felt? Relief. That's right. It was horrible – I love my wife more than anything in the world, but when she felt the most miserable pain she's ever felt, I felt relieved. Relieved that we didn't have to go through the process of raising a child. And because I felt relieved, I also felt guilt. Just an overwhelming amount of can't-sleep-at-night guilt. And with her feeling so miserable and me feeling so guilty, it almost ruined our marriage. It *did* ruin it. We're still together but things have never been the same. Eventually we moved on though. We learned to live with it. And every time a kid cuts in front of our car or we pass a newborn in a stroller, we go through it all again for a split second. And there's nothing to be done about that. And Milo, I'm sorry, but if *I* can't forget, then there's no way *you* can. We can work on coping strategies and ways to momentarily distract you from your memories. But I'm going to tell you right off the bat: I can't make you forget. All I can do is tell you what everyone else does in order to keep going and that's *repress*. Repress the hell out of your life and then lie to yourself about doing so. Otherwise all this shit is just too much to take.

(**MILO** *nods and sniffles.*)

MILO. You don't have any Armagnac do you?

HULIE. I don't but as a matter of fact I have some brandy on my shelf, which is like Armagnac.

MILO. I'll take a mouth full of that then please.

(HULIE *goes for the Brandy. Lights out.*)

Scene 7

(*The Blind Eagle.* **SAMANTHA** *sits at the bar having a glass of white wine, reading a manuscript. She shakes her leg nervously.* **TITO** *writes the specials on a blackboard nearby.* **JOEY** *walks in, wearing a light jacket over his campus security uniform.*)

TITO. (*Still writing.*) What up.

JOEY. Hey. Getting warmer out.

(**JOEY** *nods. He sees* **SAMANTHA**.)

Tito.

SAMANTHA. (*Quickly.*) I turned twenty-one last week I swear, March 16th.

TITO. Yo it's fine I checked her. (**TITO** *writes. Then he turns to* **SAMANTHA**.) I checked you right?

SAMANTHA. Yes. I swear.

TITO. (*To* **JOEY**.) It's white wine anyways.

(**JOEY** *sighs and shakes his head.*)

JOEY. Heard you got your official bouncer license. Congrats.

TITO. Yo thanks man. Turning over a new leaf of responsibility. And vigilance.

JOEY. And you guys got a beer and wine agreement or what have you?

TITO. Yeah, shitty wines though. We're also trying out some fancy schmancy food from the Rhinebeck farmer's market. Pretending to be all classy and shit to make some dough.

JOEY. Not for long. I don't know if you heard but Gina just sold the place. For real this time.

TITO. Get the fuck outta here.

JOEY. Yeah that's what *she's* doing. Getting the fuck outta here. First thing she did was book a one-way ticket to, uh Barcelona or some shit.

TITO. Damn.

> (**MILO** *enters from behind* **JOEY**.)

JOEY. *(To* **TITO**.) Hey, what's that say – "Lamb Francobolli?" What the fuck is "Francobolli?"

MILO. It's plural for "Francobollo."

> (**JOEY** *turns to* **MILO** *awkwardly.*)

JOEY. Oh. Well what's that mean?

MILO. Just "miniature." But I guess they think "Francobollo" sounds better. Tito, it's getting nice out, you should turn on the heaters out back so people can eat outside.

TITO. Look at this guy, learning to think ahead. Yo Milo it takes them a little bit to warm up, but when I get back? You, me, chess. And this time for cash money.

MILO. But I haven't played since you taught me.

TITO. So? You use the board in our show.

MILO. Not to play. You're gonna kill me.

TITO. Hey you gotta learn somehow.

> (**TITO** *exits.* **JOEY** *shakes his head at him.* **MILO** *sees* **SAMANTHA**.)

MILO. Hi.

SAMANTHA. Hey. Remember me?

MILO. How could I forget?

SAMANTHA. *(Chuckles.)* Right. *(Beat.)* Wait was that a joke?

MILO. Yeah little joke there. So you're back at Deans this semester.

SAMANTHA. Yeah they let me back. I'm on probation though. And I have to meet with the school psychiatrist 'cause of the, y'know… He has the worst B.O. *You* would really hate him actually. Y'know 'cause of the smell…

MILO. Right. Gotcha.

SAMANTHA. Anyway so, um, I just wanted to stop by to say thank you. I figured you'd be here, so…

MILO. Thank you? What for?

SAMANTHA. Well I sort of heard through the grapevine that, uh, they brought you into the disciplinary hearing about me.

MILO. Yeah, that was weird.

SAMANTHA. And that you said you believed me. About the cheating. Or *not* cheating rather.

MILO. Well I've learned to "hold my tongue" as they say. I just felt it was "inconclusive."

SAMANTHA. Right. Oh! But also I brought over this manuscript. Of Dr. Hulie's book. He said it's a "rough draft" but he wanted to run it by you first.

MILO. Oh, I could've gotten it from him at our next session.

SAMANTHA. Yeah, but I thought I could bring it over myself. Anyway, um, here.

(She hands him the manuscript.)

MILO. Well thank you, I'll go home and memorize it right away.

SAMANTHA. *(Nodding.)* Cool. Nice. *(Beat.)* Oh my God, was that another joke?

MILO. Yeah just a little one.

SAMANTHA. That was so good! Anyway I'm supposed to go meet with the school shrink like 10 minutes ago, so um…

JOEY. Oh you going back to Campus?

SAMANTHA. Yeah.

JOEY. I'll give you a lift. I gotta punch in anyway.

SAMANTHA. Oh, um, okay. Thank you.

JOEY. Yeah, y'know. *(Beat. He lingers awkwardly. He points to a wine bottle in front of* **MILO.***)* Hey what's that wine?

MILO. Yeah, looks like it.

JOEY. "Hermann J. Wiemer." Imagine if your name was Hermann J. Wiemer.

MILO. You'd probably have no friends.

JOEY. *(Chuckling.)* Yeah I know right? And look, Hermann's spelled with two N's.

MILO. *(Chuckling.)* "Her-Mannnnnn." *(Doing a nerd voice.)* Ehhh, hello, my name's Hermann with two N's. Would you please drink the wine I made in my basement.

(**JOEY** *laughs. Then exhales.*)

JOEY. Ah shit, I was blue with envy, I was.

MILO. Mmm?

JOEY. No, I'm saying you were right, I was blue, green, whatever. I just... I hate my job man. Y'know? I fucking hate it. And I just thought this shrink guy was gonna make you better and then you were gonna come back and we'd like do voices and shit together while we worked – not that you were bad and had to be fixed, but it's like working there alone? It's killing my soul. Anyway Gina and I went to your show in Poughkeepsie. I don't know if you saw us or whatever, but it was awesome. It's like weird and funny, not always intentionally, but why didn't *we* think to do that y'know? Nah, I mean, whatever. Tito's a tool but I thought he was manipulating you, and I guess he just wanted to manipulate *with* you, or something. But I just wish we would've thought of it. 'Cause you and I got a real rapport.

SAMANTHA. Um, I really need to get going.

JOEY. Right. Sorry. *(To* **MILO**.*)* Anyway, I wanna look for a new job or something. 'Cause y'know. You inspired me or whatever, so. *(He puts a hand on* **MILO**'s *shoulder and squeezes. To* **SAMANTHA**.*)* Okay, sorry, let's go.

(**JOEY** *and* **SAMANTHA** *start to exit.*)

MILO. *(Calling after him.)* You could work security at our show in Ulster. We don't really need it and we can't really pay anything. *(Beat.)* But it would be fun to have you there.

JOEY. *(Shrugs.)* Yeah maybe. I mean, assuming you buy me a beer, that could be fun.

(**GINA** *enters.*)

GINA. Oh hey Joey Broey.

JOEY. Oh hey, I gotta run to work, but I'll stop by later.

GINA. Yeah, no problem.

>(**JOEY** *and* **SAMANTHA** *exit.* **MILO** *notices something on the blackboard and goes to it.*)

You, uh, you fixing my specials?

MILO. Well it's spelled wrong, so.

>(**MILO** *picks up a rag and cleans the counter.*)

GINA. That's okay you don't have to do that. *(He keeps wiping.)* Um, so I don't know if you heard the news, but I'm, uh, leaving. I'm going to Barcelona.

MILO. Right, yeah I figured you'd be going. I just didn't know where. "Barcelona."

GINA. Yeah, I always wanted to go there. Beaches. Food. Y'know.

MILO. Right. No howl. From the wind.

GINA. *(Smiles.)* Right no howl. It's funny, I didn't think I'd ever leave and then suddenly the real-estate office called and they were like, "so hey we got an offer" I was like "I don't even care what it is just take it!" y'know? But anyway before I left I wanted to thank you for this. The uh, Topaz necklace. Joey said you got it for me, he thought I knew, and I was like, "what?!" I can't believe you went this whole time without saying anything.

MILO. Oh yeah, well I didn't really know if it was the same one 'cause I was tired at the time and my eyes were all brown and *(He stops himself.)* anyway, yeah.

GINA. Well, thank you, it's beautiful. Y'know it's funny, I was looking at it last night and it just got me thinking, like what *is* Topaz, y'know? I mean who decided it gets to be the birthstone of November? Did they just like flip a coin? Meaning gets assigned in the weirdest ways. Anyway what I'm trying to say is um, *(Chuckles.)*, is that I feel really bad about what I said to you. Y'know about how you waste your time and say meaningless shit 'cause I don't think that! I mean who am *I* to tell you what's meaningful and what's not, right? And I know you want me to stay, and I wish I could. But I can't, so before I go I wanted to make sure you knew that. 'Cause literally as soon as I got this offer yesterday –

MILO. No, two days ago.

GINA. What?

MILO. You got the offer two days ago. And then you accepted it today.

GINA. Oh right. But listen –

MILO. Otherwise I would've signed the papers this morning.

GINA. Uh what?

MILO. Y'know to buy the bar. I mean that's why I made you the offer. Or made it to the real-estate agency or whatever. I know it wasn't as much as those New York guys, but luckily my Mnemonist money coupled with the bit my mom left me was enough. Well without the liquor license. What I'll do with a bar with no liquor license, I don't really know. But I'll figure it out. I was just worried it wouldn't be enough for you to leave and get settled in. I mean you gotta factor in food too, y'know. You sure it was enough with food factored in?

GINA. Ye – *(She clears her throat.)* Um, yes.

MILO. Anyway this counter's really dirty and I want this place clean from now on.

GINA. I can't believe that you – Milo I can't let you do this.

MILO. Mmm, it's sort of too late already. But anyway, what were you saying about Topaz and…well I don't know, you were sort of rambling there.

GINA. I was saying… I was saying I'm gonna miss you. And *(She starts picking at his shirt.)* and I don't know, maybe before I go we could –

(She goes to kiss him. He pulls away.)

MILO. Whoa. I thought we couldn't do that anymore.

GINA. Well I… I was thinking maybe just a little, y'know? Just one last memory sort of thing?

MILO. No, I don't really want that anymore. You're leaving soon anyway.

GINA. Yeah but *(Picks at his shirt again.)* what are we supposed to do until then, around the *(Chuckles.)* the one-night cheap hotels and sawdust oyster shells.

MILO. *(Chuckles.)* What? The what?

GINA. Y'know from Alfred Prufrock. Excuse me, the *Love Song Of Alfred Prufrock.*

MILO. I don't know what you're talking about.

GINA. The poem, Milo. C'mon you're joking right? You don't forget anything.

MILO. Oh, actually – yeah so you know how sometimes I write stuff down and then throw it away? It's how I'm able to forget things like grocery lists and stuff? Yeah well Dr. Hulie made me try it out for some poems and things I learned. That might've been one of them. I mean it must've been one of them. 'Cause I don't know what you're talking about.

GINA. Right, I've, uh, I've seen you do that.

MILO. Yeah it's something I do sometimes for stuff that's not that important.

GINA. Oh. Right. Well um *(She looks away.)* I gotta run now and get my stuff packed up before I go but if I don't see you, send me your book okay?

> *(She exits.* **MILO** *stares at the door.* **TITO** *enters with a chessboard. The wind howls.)*

TITO. Damn you hear that?

MILO. Yeah turn on the oldies station, will you? It helps me think better.

> *(He turns on the radio. They start playing as* **TITO** *talks.)*

TITO. Oh hey so you know that cute girl I was talking to at the last show? Turns out she's got a roommate or a sister or something. Tomorrow night, you interested? And don't say no 'cause I know you ain't doing nothing.

Nothing but memorizing a bunch of meaningless old shit.

MILO. *(As he plays.)* I grow old, I grow old... I shall wear the bottoms of my trousers rolled.

TITO. Huh?

MILO. Nothing, just some meaningless shit from our show. *(He moves his piece.)* Checkmate.

> *(Lights out. The wind howls.)*

The End